BILLY BOB BUTTONS is the multi-award winning author of thirteen children's books including the Rubery Book Award FINALIST, Felicity Brady and the Wizard's Bookshop, the much loved The Gullfoss Legends, TOR Assassin Hunter, TOR Wolf Rising, the Cool Kids Book Prize WINNER, Wide Awake, the hysterical Muffin Monster and the UK People's Book Prize WINNER, I Think I Murdered Miss.

He is also a PATRON OF READING.

Born in the Viking city of York, he and his wife, Therese, a true Swedish girl from the IKEA county of Småland, now live in Stockholm and London. Their twin girls, Rebecca and Beatrix, and little boy, Albert, inspire Billy Bob every day to pick up a pen and work on his books.

When not writing, he enjoys tennis and playing 'MONSTER!' with his three children.

DROWNING FISH

Billy Bob Buttons

the WISHING SHELF press

the WISHING SHELF press

Published by THE WISHING SHELF PRESS, UK.
ISBN 978 1523346813
www.bbbuttons.co.uk Twitter @BillyBobButtons
Printed and bound by Book Printing UK.
Edited by Alison Emery, Therese Råsbäck and
Svante Jurnell.

To Lloyd,

Enjoy the book,

For

REBECCA

J A P A N

4th October, 1227 A.D.

The tips of the two swords meet and Fury is on me. He is brutal, his blade a blur and I step hastily back, tumbling over a barrel.

Gentlemanly, the sorcerer steps off, allowing me to find my feet; and, over by the wall, Felix, a skinny boy with spots, trumpets his approval at my clumsy footwork and poor swordsmanship. I feel a fool. A silly schoolgirl in a classroom full of scholars.

'If you wish to be a Seeker, you must first

know the skills of the ninja,' Fury tells me.

'Why?' I hiss. I lift my sword, determined to do better.

'To find the children of Ammit, you must excel in Kenjutsu, the sword, kyujutsu, the bow, yarijutsu, the spear and bojutsu, the stick. You must climb a cliff, jump a river and get free of a prison in seconds. All skills of the ninja.'

'Forget it,' sneers Felix, his words low and gravelly. 'She'll never be a Seeker. She's only ten. Best to feed her to the Glumsnappers.'

'We will see,' says the sorcerer. He attacks but I shoulder him off me, twirl my wrist and thrust. Our swords spark and, just for a second, I see a way in. But I stop; I don't want to hurt him. Then, to my horror, I suddenly feel cold steel under my own chin.

Slowly, I lower my sword.

'You remind me of a doddery old woman with a broom,' he mocks me. He too lowers his sword. But I think he knows I had him. Just for a second. I can tell by the arch of the eyebrows, the stony set of his jaw. Oh yes, he knows. 'But there is a hunger in you, Isabella. I can see it.' He shoots me the jackal's eye. 'Skill too, I see.'

He drops low, his foot sweeping my off my feet and I cartwheel to the floor. Swiftly, I lift my sword but it is torn from my fist.

He drops to a knee and eyes me keenly. Stubbornly, I return his look. 'Do you wish to be the best?' he says simply.

Felix titters and rolls his eyes. 'She's just a silly girl,' he scoffs.

I eye the boy coldly and he shuts up. 'Yes,

Master,' I say looking back at Fury. 'Very much.'

'Good.' He helps me to my feet. 'This here,' he flutters his hand at the papery walls, 'is Hornet Temple. Here, in this forgotten century, I will show you the ways of the ninja. If, over the next three months, you do everything – EVERYTHING – I tell you to do, you WILL be the best Seeker in the Sorcerer's Covern.'

'Except for you,' I say, brushing dust off my kimono.

He nods, the corners of his thin lips curling up. 'Except for me,' he agrees.

YESTERDAY

Chapter 1

DORFMORON SNOT

My mind will not let me sleep. I tumble over and over in my bed, my sheets twisted and knotted. In my tortured mind, I see Sinjin Fury's tomb-like eyes, cold and pitch-black. Then, just for a split second...

THE BUS

It looms over me, a horror film of filthy windows, crooked bumpers and blood-splattered wheels. A bus from the pits of hell.

I see...

I see...

SINJIN FURY'S ARMY

The Woolly Glumsnappers, the hulking Dorfmorons and the terrifying Shubablybubs. All claws, guffaws and fang-filled jaws. Hundreds of them, all jumbled up in my skull. Like me, they tumble over and over...

'MOP!' I yell. My eyes fly open and I sit up sharply in my bed.

The wizard sitting on a stool by my elbow jumps up too. 'It's OK, Isabella,' he says soothingly. Kindly, he plumps up my pillows and pulls my blanket up over my knees. 'Rufus is here.'

I look at him, blinking wildly. 'Where's Simon?' I demand.

'I don't know,' he answers simply. 'Nobody knows. But, we'll find him. Trust me.'

I swallow a hundred 'whys, wheres, whos and whens' and return my red curls to the hill of pillows. I see I'm back in Clodcorn Windmill, Seeker HQ. Old, wonky timbers criss-cross the roof and, over by the wall, there is a tractor with rusty, yellow hubcaps. For just over six months, when the school bell rung, this is where I'd returned to. Here, in this old windmill perched on a hill just north of Trotswood, my pretend family and I plotted and planned, trying to find a way to discover if Simon truly had the gift; the gift to kill with a wish.

Stretching my body, I yelp in agony. I peer under the blanket to see my left pyjama leg is rolled up to my thigh and my knee is swollen and red. It throbs mercilessly. It seems, even with my Seeker skills, I'd been no match for Sinjin Fury. I remember bitterly how he'd crushed me with just a tiny flick of his wand. But it is not the only thing I remember...

'What day is it?' I ask Rufus.

The wizard sniffs and pulls a hanky from his pocket. He is lollipop-skinny with three wispy

14

curls clinging stubbornly to his well-polished skull. Dressed in a scarlet silk tunic and a lumpy pelican-pink cravat, he reminds me of a circus clown. But he's not. He's my boss.

'This old windmill must be crawling with germs,' he says.

I scowl. What is he not telling me? 'Rufus!'

'Hmm?'

'Answer me,' I persist.

Winching up his chin, he surveys me with his gloomy, redsetter eyes. 'Thursday,' he says.

'THURSDAY!' I try to sit up.

'You were in a coma,' he informs me soberly. 'You were very badly hurt and your knee's still a scrambled mess.'

'But, if it's Thursday, then it's been six days...'

'Thirteen.'

'Sorry?'

'Thirteen days.'

I look at him in horror. 'So the crash and my battle with Sinjin Fury...'

'Two weeks tomorrow.'

'My God,' I murmur. Two weeks! I feel numb; so numb, I wonder, for a second, how I can possibly exist. I remember Anthony, the boy crushed by the...

'So Simon, he's Loki. The son of...' I swallow; it's difficult to say.

'Ammit. Yes, we think so.' He sits silently, twiddling his thumbs, then, 'You were pretty badly hurt so I took you here, to Clodcorn Windmill, to recover.'

I nod my thanks. 'Do you - do you think Fury's captured him?' I stumble.

16

'To be honest, we don't know where Simon is. But my gut tells me no.'

I chew on my lip and nod, a sharp jerk of my neck. I think the wizard's gut is right. I don't know how I know. I just do. 'Who's looking for him?'

'Everybody,' he answers cheerily. He hops to his feet. 'I think I'll pop the kettle on. And I must dust too. It's so terribly...'

'Who's everybody?' I butt in. I know Rufus often keeps stuff from me and I know why, but my knee hurts terribly and I'm in no mood for secrets.

Reluctantly, he sits back down. 'Well, there's Jagger Steel, he's on the hunt up north. Jub Jub, he's west of here.' The wizard frowns and chews his lip. 'I think he's in Spittle on the Bog. Oh, and

17

there's Cody Blitz too and he's, er, well, I don't know where he is.' He ticks them off on his fingers. 'They'll find the boy.'

With a deep scowl, I nod. Steel's a moron and not on my Christmas card list but, still, he's a competent Seeker; and so is Jub Jub. As for Cody Blitz, he's the best there is. When he's not guzzling sherry. But do I trust them to find Simon? I lost him, not them. He's my responsibility.

I throw off my cover and look crossly at my swollen knee. I must help them. But how? I can't even walk. I try to think but it's as if my mind's a can of Spam and I need a tin opener to get into it. The only thing I can think of...

Shrewdly, I eye the old wizard. He's the best alchemist I know. He can even brew a Sleep

Tonic from worms and viper venom. For six months he's pretended to be my dad. He knows me and I know him. I think he respects me; trusts me. But will he help?

'Rufus, I wonder if...'

'No.'

'But...'

'Izzy,' he growls, clambering to his feet, 'just try to rest.'

'I CAN'T!' I storm. I rub my eyes with a balled-up fist. Everything is so complicated. I'm often tempted to just run away. Run away till I get to Lands End. 'I know Fury,' I say.

'Nobody knows him better,' mutters Rufus, his eyes to his silver-buckled boots.

I nod. Will he ever fully trust me, I wonder. Will any of them? 'Yes, nobody knows him better,' I admit. 'So I know how evil he is and I know, if he finds Simon, he'll end up being the most powerful wizard in the world. Then what will he do? Who will he kill? Nobody will be safe. I must stop him, Rufus.'

'Izzy...'

'It happened on my watch. You can fix my knee. I know you can.'

Just then, the door to the windmill ricochets off the wall and a tubby man with a crew cut and red, welty skin, thunders in. It is Cody Blitz, the Seeker.

'We think he's in Scotland,' he pants, skidding to an untidy halt.

Rufus, who'd pulled his wand, slips it back in his pocket. 'Who?' he snaps. 'Simon or Sinjin Fury?'

'Simon.' Cody flips me a wink. 'Jagger Steel spotted him in Devil's Ash. It's a tiny town a mile from Inverness.'

'I know where it is,' mutters Rufus irritably. He rubs his bristly chin. 'And Sinjin Fury? Did Steel spot him too?'

'No.' He frowns. 'But there's been a report of a storm just to the west of there. It will soon hit Devil's Ash. It must be him.'

'Why must it?' I ask.

'There's no wind,' he answers simply.

I swallow. Wherever the wizard sets foot, a thunder storm proceeds him. But there's never any wind; not even a gust. 'Then he must know Simon's there too,' I say, a tiny tremor to my words. I look beseechingly to Rufus. 'Help me,' I implore him. 'Fix my knee.'

'Izzy, I don't think...'

I hook my fingers on his silk tunic. 'JUST DO IT!'

'We do need her,' chips in Cody. 'She knows Fury's tactics and, anyway, if Simon only sees me or Jagger, he'll panic and scarper. But if he sees Izzy here...'

'He trusts me,' I say vehemently 'I just spent six months with him. If he sees me, there's no way he'll run.'

Rufus chomps for a second on his lower lip. I can almost see the cogs in his skull spinning. 'OK, OK,' he finally says. Ballooning his cheeks, he totters over to a dusty shelf by my bed and picks up a bottle. 'This will help. But, remember, it will not mend the knee. It'll just mask the, er...'

'Throbbing agony?' I suggest.

He nods. Then, uncorking it, he tips the contents over my injured leg.

'Gross,' I cry, screwing up my nose. 'It looks like snot.'

'It is,' says the wizard, evenly. 'It's Dorfmoron snot.'

'Em, sorry? Dorfmoron...'

'Snot, yes.'

'Look!' yelps Cody, excitedly. 'There's a lumpy bit.'

Lost for words, I let the wizard drench my knee in the slimy goo. 'How's it feeling now?' he finally asks.

'Sticky,' I reply sourly.

'It looks revolting,' says Cody, who seems to be in a very helpful sort of mood. I suspect he's been to the pub.

'Yes, it is,' agrees Rufus with a hint of a smile, 'but it'll do the job. For now, anyway,' he adds. He stoppers the bottle. 'Go on, try it.'

Gritting my teeth, I swing my feet off the bed and rest them on the windmill's cold floor. Then I slowly stand up. 'Wow!' I cry, hopping up and down. 'I can't feel a thing.'

'The Dorfmoron snot will not fix the knee,' Rufus reminds me soberly. 'It will just numb it. Do too much on it and, well...'

'I'll limp forever?'

He nods. 'And for openers, I'd stop hopping.'

'Oh! Yes, sorry.'

'Remember Izzy, Seekers must be fit and swift of foot. There's no room in this job for a witch with a limp. If you hurt your knee permanently, your career will be over.'

24

'There's always The Wishing Shelf,' suggests Cody. 'The boss there, Felicity Brady, she's looking for workers.'

'Me! Work in a magic bookshop,' I sneer. 'No way.' I shoot him a cold look. He knows a Seeker is all I ever wanted to be. I turn to the dresser by my bed. I expect to see my wand on it but it's not there. With a scowl, I slip my hand under my pillow. 'Where's my wand?' I ask.

'Sorry Izzy,' says Cody, stepping up to me. 'Fury destroyed it.' He pulls a stubby-looking stick from his pocket and hands it to me. 'Here. This is my back-up. It's not very flashy but, well – it'll do the job.'

I nod slowly. I can smell sherry on him. 'Thanks,' I muster. I loved my wand but I'm determined not to show them I'm upset. Almost every Seeker's a boy so, to get respect, I must be the best; and, anyway, I do not need anybody's pity. 'So, how do we get there?' I quiz them.

'We fly,' answers Cody with a grin.

I eye him grumpily. The Seekers preferred method of getting from A to B is, sadly, not by helicopter or super-sonic jet. 'If we must,' I mutter. 'OK! All set? Let's go.'

But the two Seekers just stand there chuckling.

'What's so funny?' I demand, my fists on my hips. Then it dawns on me and I look down. 'Oh,' I mutter, my cheeks reddening. I'm still in my pyjamas.

'OK,' I say. 'Let's get tooled up.'

J A P A N

5th October, 1227 A.D.

By the look of his eyes, Fury must be Japanese, with a stern crew cut and the beefy biceps of a smithy. He walks on the pads of his feet, a panther on the hunt, his short legs swirling up his robe and the sword on his belt. 'This, Isabella, is the ninja short bow.' Fury holds it up for me to see. 'It is only three feet from tip to tip but with it you can hit a bumble bee from a hundred and fifty feet, a cow's udder from three hundred.'

Three hundred feet; not too shabby, but I still prefer my trusty wand. Thoughtfully, I finger the bow...

'Fish bone,' he correctly answers my frown, 'in three segments so it can be dismantled and hidden in a pocket.'

I look to his devil-black eyes and shiver, a chill creeping up from my boots to my belly. He has the eyes of a butcher. 'A handy toy,' I mutter, wondering if the sorcerer did indeed just see into my mind.

Noting my tone, he looks to me with hooked eyebrows. 'Very,' he says, twirling a red-spotted umbrella.

Sorry, Master.' I put my hands up in mock surrender. 'It just seems a little, you know, old school for a Seeker.'

Fury responds with a tut. 'The quiver, or rimenkya in Japanese, can hold up to twelve arrows,' he ploughs on, 'and slips tidily over the shoulder.' He shows me.

The boy, Felix, who seems to be my new 'keeper', had woken me to a chilly dawn with a kick of his steel-capped boot. I did not sleep well, my mind full of burning beds and melting flesh. So, still rubbing my eyes, I had been led out to the lawns.

There, in the shadow of Hornet Temple, I had been met by Fury, and, with the yellow clouds curdling and thinning and with the sun peeking cheekily over the hills, my schooling in archery, kyajutsu in Japanese, had begun.

I peer over at the temple. The walls tower over me and look almost unclimbable and the

29

door looks to be two feet thick. The roof is no better. It is covered in red tile and drops steeply to a curly, flipped-up rim. The rim, I see, is lined with a row of barbed thorns.

It is a fortress, I think dejectedly. But, then, why worry? I'm an orphan lost in history. There's nowhere for me to run too.

Our only company seems to be the birds in the trees and the hum of insects, so I ask Fury if I'm his only student.

He nods. 'It is spring in Japan now. The ryu, school you call it, is shut until December.'

'So you opened your doors just for me,' I chide him. 'I'm flattered.'

'Don't be.' His lips hint of a smile. 'The Sorcerer's Covern pays me well to babysit new students.'

So, he thinks I'm just a 'baby'. Well, I'll show him.

Reluctantly, I return to the archery lesson. A hundred whys, whos, wheres and whens twirl in my mind, but I'm too frightened to push my luck. 'It's a well-crafted tool,' I admit, 'but I much prefer the accuracy of my wand.'

In a flash, he slips an arrow from the quiver, swiftly fits it to the string of the bow and lets it fly. A rosy red plum on a far off tree thumps to the lawn, effectively ending my protests.

'Do not be fooled by the simplicity of the bow. 'Here, you try.' He steps up to me and with a tiny encouraging nod, offers me the bow and the quiver of arrows.

With a cynical frown, I take the bow and arrows. I can feel Felix's critical eyes on me; I think he's hoping I will miss.

Clumsily, I try to fit the butt of the bamboo arrow to the string, but Fury stops me.

'Remember, a Seeker must always be prepared to flee the coop. So, bend your back knee.' He shows me and begrudgingly I mirror him. 'Good. Now, if necessary, you can push off your back foot and run for the hills.'

I nod. This is sort of fun so I decide to show off.

With the string well past my cheekbone and the arrow level with my eye, I target the plum tree and shoot, but the arrow ricochets off a banana tree almost a hundred feet short.

The boy, Felix, snorts and begins to slow clap but a withering look from Fury quickly stops him.

A little crestfallen, I lower the bow.

'Isabella, the bow is very different to the wand. A spell is direct; the arrow is not. You must remember to allow for the curve of the arrow's path.'

I nod curtly. 'Yes, Master.'

'For every 1,000 arrows you shoot, you will improve by 1 percent. Only 99,999 to go, Isabella.' He frowns. 'No, I think I'll call you Izzy. Yes, much better. He bows. 'Keep up the good work, Izzy. I will return soon.'

He pads off and I'm left under the watchful eye of Felix.

I spend the rest of the day working on my archery skills, stopping only for a pithy lunch: a bowl of beef and rice, my second in two days, and a cup of lemony spring water. It is surprisingly hot in the October sun, the blustery wind doing a miserable job of chilling the droplets on my brow. Nevertheless, Felix's sentry duty is unwavering; a pit bull watching over a rabbit hole.

By sunset there is a nasty welt on my finger but I'm happy to see twenty or so plums littering the lawn.

My tutor, Fury, walks back over. He looks to my chaffed hand and the nest of plums and nods. 'Bravo, Izzy. I'm happy to see there will be plum crumble for supper.'

He twists sharply on his heel and strolls off, but not back to the temple. I suspect he expects me to follow him, so I do, my shadow, Felix, doggedly on my heels

It is, I must admit, very pretty here. Over a dozen richly tinted flower beds litter the trimmed lawn and, in a corner, by a stone sundial, a yellow rose cheekily climbs the trunk of the banana tree my errant arrow had hit. We amble by nests of soft-tongued orchids, lofty bamboo trees and hundreds and hundreds of blossoming chrysanthemums.

But many of the flowers I simply do not know; I enjoy drawing and my fingers itch to sketch them.

'Izzy, did you know, and not many do, there must be well over two hundred different plants that can kill? Two hundred! Amazing, I know. You might find the venom in the petals, the stems, the tubers, the roots, or even the bark. Why, in these very flower beds you will discover the sweet perfume of the hemlock, the deceptively pretty petals of the monkshood and, look, over there, the red berry of the cuckoo-pint. Very nasty customers and, trust me, not so innocent. But such plants can be effective tools in the hands of the Seeker.'

'A coward's way to kill,' I murmur.

'Izzy, Izzy, the ninja did not invent the clever ploy of murdering the enemy in his bed. The Thugs of Kali did in the 8th century followed by Hassan of Iraq and his fanatics in the 11th. You see, the assassin is part of our history, our world culture. Remember, a Seeker's job is to find the children of Ammit and destroy them.'

'Not THEM,' I correct him, 'We destroy what's IN them.'

He shrugs. 'This,' he fingers the petals of the monkshood, 'might be the only way of doing it.'

Twaddle, I think, my temper spiking. He seems

to be confusing the work of a Seeker with the cowardly work of a ninja. Yes, to be a Seeker I need the ninja's skills, but I don't need the ninja's work ethic. However, I keep my lips tightly shut.

We stroll by the tree I spent the day attacking and I scoop a plum up off the grass. It is shiny and plump but, when I chew on it, the yellow flesh is surprisingly bitter.

'In Italy in the 16th century,' Fury persists, 'a lady, Madonna Teofania di Adamo, discovered the cure to the problem of 'annoying husbands'. She actually sold her 'medicine' in shops.' He barks a laugh. 'The result, six hundred fewer husbands and six hundred happy widows in the world.'

We stop by the pond and I look casually down at the swampy-looking water.

'Jump it,' Fury says.

Momentarily lost for words, I spit pulped plum on a firecracker bush. 'What?' I finally muster.

'THE POND!' he trumpets, grinding his heel in the grass. The tip of his umbrella sparks. It must be his wand. 'Jump it,' he tells me sternly.

I look to the muddy pool, my eyes narrowing. 'You must be joking,' I protest. 'It's over twenty feet.'

'Firstly, I never joke,' he tells me stiffly, 'and, secondly, you think too much. Whether it is possible or not is not important. Think only, I must jump this pond, I will jump this pond. Only then will you succeed.'

I back up a little. Then, clenching my teeth, I sprint for the bank. I jump, pulling my knees up to my chin. Nine feet, ten feet...

I hit the water with a tremendous splash.

I look up to see Fury, the ghost of a smile on his lips. Felix, however, is bent over, hooting and cackling so much I wonder if, perhaps, he is having an asthma attack.

The sorcerer pulls a hip flask from the pocket of his robe and drinks from it. Then he twists on his sandaled heels and, whistling a cheery tune, he strolls off. 'Keep up, Izzy, plum crumble for supper.'

It seems, I ponder, up to my knees in slimy pond weed and lily pads, that Fury enjoys a good joke after all.

Chapter 2

THE CRUSTY CRYPT

With a deep scowl, I peer over the top of the Landrover's bonnet. The Crusty Crypt Inn is twenty feet back from the street, dimly lit by a flickering lamp over the porch. It is eleven o'clock and the moon is up. But I suspect it will soon be hidden. To the west, a storm rolls over the hills. Thunder booms and lightning splits the sky. Sinjin Fury will soon be here.

I turn to Jagger Steel, the Seeker, and, for a

second, I eye his gigantic shoulders, bulldog jaw and long, spindly fingers; they look all wrinkly as if he'd pickled them in brine. 'Simon's in there?' I quiz him. 'But why? He's only eleven?'

'He works there,' he tells me dismissively, his yellow-tarnished teeth working on a lump of gum. 'I think he's the cook.'

Cook! I'm surprised Simon even knows how to. He is, to be honest, a very odd sort of boy. Obsessed by Star Trek, he's a loner with the IQ of a chemistry professor and the temper of a troll with tooth rot. I remember how upset he'd been when I'd told him his model of the Starship Enterprise reminded me of a dustbin lid. But now he's a cook! My eyebrows lift; it seems I misjudged him.

Cody Blitz and Rufus scurry over and drop

down by the car's wheel. 'We checked the street and the roofs and everything looks OK,' whispers Rufus. 'No Glumsnappers anyway.'

I nod, ballooning my cheeks. 'Good,' I say with feeling.

'Horrid monsters, Glumsnappers,' comments Steel.

'It's the teeth,' says Cody. 'So bloody sharp.'

'Oh, I don't know,' I say nonchalantly. 'For me, it's the acid blood. It's a devil to get off.' I wink at Rufus. 'So, what's the plan, Boss?'

The Seeker's eyes narrow, then, 'Cody, Steel and I will stay here. We'll keep watch for Fury and his Glumsnappers.'

'And his Dorfmorons,' adds Cody.

And his Shubablybubs,' pips in Steel with a mocking curl of his lips.

42

I swallow. The Shubablybubs frighten me the most. Yellow eyeballs, car crusher jaws and teeth the size of a killer sharks. Good job I'm fully kitted up in my steel-woven dress, my steel-capped boots buckled up to my knees. I check the Seeker tools hooked to my belt. Firstly, my skull bombs, just twist and toss. Then, my pumpkin lantern, steel-shelled, the candle a potent mix of wax and gunpowder. Blindingly bright.

Bring 'em on, I think with a smirk. 'And what do I do?' I ask Rufus, who's similarly tooled up – except for the dress.

The wizard eyes me for a second. 'This boy, Simon, he trusts you, yes?'

'Yes.'

'Good. Then off y' trot.'

'Sorry?'

'Go fetch him, stupid,' mutters Steel with a roll of his eyes.

'Oh, right.' Shooting the bulldog-jawed Seeker a cold look, I jump to my feet. Then I pull my lantern off my belt and, very slowly, I creep up the street to the Crusty Crypt Inn.

'Remember, Izzy,' calls Rufus, 'show the demon who's boss.'

I smile. 'I will,' I murmur, not bothering to look back.

The storm is much closer now, the thunder rattling the windows, lightning splitting the sky. I slip by a ramshackle cottage with a crumbling mossy wall. On it, a cat sits hissing at a bird in a tree. The only street lamp flickers and blinks off. Is it trying to warn me, I wonder, like a lighthouse warning a ship to stay away from the rocks.

I stop by a bin, the stench of rotten fish wafting up my nostrils. For a second, I hunker down there, my eyes fixed on the pub's red door. ABBA's Super Trooper is playing and, in the window, I spot a man chomping nuts and laughing.

It seems there's nothing to be frightened off.

I blow out the lantern and hook it back on my dress. It's pitch-black on the street now but I no longer need it. My Seeker blood is now flowing through me. Suddenly, I feel much sharper and I can see better than a barn owl.

I jump to my feet...

'I see you, Seeker.' A sharp, acid-laced whisper stabs my mind.

I freeze, the lantern on my hip swaying like a pendulum, dripping wax on my boots.

'Trying to stop me, little girl?'

'No, I...'

'Trying to hurt me?'

I say nothing. Like a lasso, the words drag on my feet, commanding me to turn and flee. But I'm rooted to the street. It's as if my legs no longer work.

'Who – who's there?' I muster, a nervy jitter distorting my words.

The seconds tick ponderously by but there's no answer. But I know who it is. Sinjin Fury! He's in me; invading my skull. To him, my mind is just a toy. A toy he very much enjoys playing with. Gritting my teeth, I command my legs to work and, slowly, tiny step by tiny step, I stagger on.

I creep over to the door of the Crusty Crypt Inn and, very softly, press my fingertips to the mildewed wood. Then, very slowly, I push it open.

The pub reeks of beer, smelly feet and Cheesy Wotsit crisps. It is stuffy too, packed to the rafters with crumpled old men and hikers in need of a bed. In a dimly lit corner, two men play pool. On the floor, by a hill of glowing embers, a redsetter chews his paws. And, over by the bar, is Simon Spittle.

There is a sudden hush. Everybody is now staring at me. It seems the customers of the Crusty Crypt Inn don't often see girls with steel-capped boots, and in a dress festooned with skull bombs and pumpkin lanterns. 'She must be French,' a man in the corner mutters.

It seems only Simon hasn't spotted me.

Typical. So I stroll over to him. It feels odd to see him here in the Crusty Crypt Inn in Devil's Ash. I know I just spent six months with him but then I only suspected he was a son of Ammit. In Trotswood, I'd enjoyed being with him; his silly, oddly charming ways. But now I know he IS a son of Ammit, everything feels different. Now, there's no room for sentiment. Now – he's just my job.

And my job is to escort Simon to Gullfoss, to the Sorcerer's Covern and, there, they will perform the Eliminus Ceremony. The boy's powers will be destroyed and Fury's plan – whatever it is – will be scuppered.

But Simon must never know any of this. The ceremony is risky. To him, anyway. If he were to suspect, he'd probably run. And, to be honest, he'd be foolish not to.

'Hello, Mop,' I say, stopping in front of him. I sort of want to hug him but Simon's not a big fan of hugs. In fact, the No Hug Rule is his No. 1 Rule. And, anyway, there's a sticky-looking bar in the way.

He looks at me and his eyes narrow. Then he says, 'Drink?'

'Em.' I scowl; not what I'd been expecting. 'Mop, it's me, Isabella.'

He frowns.

'You know. Isabella. Pretty girl, big fan of Star, er – is it Wars?'

'Trek. It's Star TREK!' He sighs. 'Yes, I remember. My IQ is over a hundred and fifty.'

'Mop, listen to me. We think Sinjin Fury's on his way here. We must...'

'He is,' he says lightly.

'Sorry?' My eyes skip fretfully to the pub's door and I step closer to the bar.

'Don't be sorry. I'm very clever. I just know stuff. My IQ is a hundred and...'

'Fifty. Yes, I know.'

He looks at a clock on the wall. 'He'll be here in 237 seconds from, er – now. No, no, sorry. From now.'

My jaw drops. Simon's timing him! How is it, whenever I see this boy, I feel totally wrong-footed?

Discreetly, I slip my wand from my pocket. 'So let's scarper,' I hiss, trying my very best to recover.

'Sorry, I can't. I work here. My job's to sell drinks to the Crusty Crypt Inn customers. Nuts and Cheesy Wotsits too. Doris, the landlady, she's in the cellar by the way,' he nods to a trapdoor by his feet and I see the lid is up, 'she told me the Wotsits fell off the back of a lorry. Odd. The box isn't ripped or dented. My shift ends at eleven thirty so I can't 'scarper' till then.' He turns to the man by my elbow. 'Drink?'

The man nods. 'Pint of bitter,' he says gruffly.

'Nuts?'

'No.'

'Cheesy Wotsits?'

'No!'

'Pity.'

Puzzled, I study him as he pulls the fellow's pint of beer. He's tall for eleven; skinny too with messy curls and sickly-yellow cheeks. He looks a little bedraggled; there is dirt on his cheek and

51

his jumper is grubby and torn. But he looks surprisingly well for a kid on the run. Confident even. Different.

He hands the man his frothy drink. 'Three fifty,' he says.

'Bloody rip off,' mutters back the man, dropping a fiver on the bar top.

'Nuts?'

The man scowls at him, 'What did you call me?'

'Nuts? Do you want any?'

'No I bloody don't.'

'Cheesy Wotsits then? They fell off the back of a lorry.'

'Y' pulling my leg?' the man growls.

Simon's eyes widen innocently. 'Don't be silly,' he says. 'Your leg's down there and I'm up here.'

I roll my eyes. No, he's still the boy I remember. A loony with the ability to upset a bishop.

'Mop,' I interrupt them, 'we must...'

'Hold on.' He thumps a key on the cash till and the drawer pings open. Then he hands the man his change. He turns to me. 'Now, what can I get you? Nuts?'

'I don't want any...'

'Cheesy Wotsits then? Or there's Monster Munch...'

'MOP!'

'There's only one fifty here,' the man butts in. 'I handed you a tenner.'

Simon scowls at him. 'No, you handed me a fiver.'

'Tenner.'

'Fiver.'

'Tenner.'

'Fiver.'

'Mop,' I hiss.

'I'm not going to be conned by a skinny kid with spots,' yells the man.

'And I'm not going to be conned by a moron who's so stupid he'd try to kill a bird by throwing it off a cliff.'

I shut my eyes and sigh.

The man jumps to his feet. 'Why, you cheeky little...'

But his torrent of angry words is lost when six oddly-clad monsters suddenly plod in the door. Drenched in armour and capped with horned helmets, the ferrety-eyed monsters growl and hiss, stamping studded boots on the beer-splattered floor. 'Glumsnappers,' I mutter. With a grunt, I pocket my wand. My magic will not work. The enchanted steel protecting them will stop any of my spells.

For a long, long second, everybody in the Crusty Crypt just looks at the Glumsnappers in horror. Then, a man in a kilt drops his Cheesy Wotsits and sprints for the door, the rest of the pub's customers – and the redsetter – hot on his flapping heels.

'Monsters,' mutters Simon darkly, stepping back. I wonder, for a split second, if he's going to try to run for it too. But, it seems, Simon is no longer the boy I remember. He picks up a fluffy duster, jumps over the bar and, together, we stand and face them.

Warily, I eye the throng of monsters, noting

the toothy jaws and the rhino-sized horns. Where the hell is Rufus, I wonder, and the rest of the Seekers.

Slowly, the Glumsnappers creep closer.

'Not good,' comments Simon in a surprisingly sunny tone.

'You seem surprisingly - chipper,' I mutter. I eye the duster clutched in his fist. 'Do you plan on tickling them till they beg for mercy?'

'No,' he says snootily. 'And, yes, I'm in excellent spirits. I get it now; my powers. So, when I spotted the storm coming I simply did the logical thing. I wished for Sinjin Fury to be hit by a bus. I suspect, any second now, the Number 10 from Inverness will jump the curb and knock him over.'

'Oh.'

'Oh?'

'Terrible news, Mop. It's not going to work. Not on Fury. He's got magical blood in him.'

'But...'

In a flurry of wolfish barks, they charge. I duck under a sweeping sword, twist and thump my attacker ruthlessly in the stomach. Wheezing, he bends over and I wallop the back of his skull with my elbow.

Thankfully, Fury, my old master, showed me how to fight with my fists too.

Simon, I see, is still on his feet fending off two of the enemy. Pretty impressive considering he's doing it with a fluffy duster! I hurry over to help him but then a second Glumsnapper jumps me. This fellow is colossal with the stumpy legs of a rhino. His sword sweeps up, grazing the cleft of my chin. I scurry back but he doggedly follows me, jabbing relentlessly for my chest. He is a hunter and he can smell my blood. I block his thrusts and, with a howl of fury, I suddenly step up to him and push him up and over the bar. He plummets to the cellar below.

The swish of steel and I instinctively duck, a shimmering sword skewering the wall by my shoulder. My third attacker yanks on the hilt trying to wrench it free but it is jammed in the timber.

In the past, I'd do the monster the civility of stepping off; he'd been unlucky and that is no way to win a fight. But not now. Not today. Today, I pull off his helmet and cuff him brutally on the jaw.

A volcano spits and growls in my chest,

pummelling my rib cage. I see my blurred eyes in the back of the blade. They burn yellow and fervently I look for the next Glumsnapper to brawl.

My eyes flit to Simon. I spot a monster slumped by his feet but the second is doing considerably better, handling his sword with expert hands. I can tell Simon is tiring and a fluffy duster is no match for steel. I must help him or he'll be captured.

'Throw the sword.' Fury is back. He knows my instincts, my primal instincts. *'Be all you can be,'* he bellows in my skull. *'Throw it now!'*

So I do. I pull the sword from the barrel, the outstretched blade quivering in fury and, with all the venom I can muster, I let fly. It tomahawks over the bar, hitting Simon's attacker with such

59

ferocity, he is thrown twenty feet, landing with a bone-crunching thud on the floor.

With rage simmering under my skin, I storm over to the body. I must...

'Yes. Yes, you must.'

...claw open his chest. Gnaw on his ribs.

'Don't forget the liver. It's full of iron and it will keep you strong.'

I must...

'Feed on him!'

I drop to my knees and rip open the Glumsnapper's tunic. But then, new words spiral in my mind. Softer. Dampening the fury. It is Ogun. His words block Sinjin's playful temptings and, slowly, I slump to the floor.

'Isabella,' yells Simon. He limps over to me, dropping to his knees.

'Run,' I whisper. 'Fetch help.'

'Help? But who do I...'

'Splinter. Find Rufus Splinter.'

'But I don't know where to...'

'GO!' I holler.

He nods and runs over to the door. 'STOP!' I suddenly cry.

He turns and scowls at me. 'Stop, go, stop, go. I'm not a bloody traffic light.'

'He's here.'

'Where?'

I nod at the door. 'Here.'

Suddenly, a woman pops up from behind the bar. 'Simon,' she yells, 'Where the hell's my customers?'

It must be Doris, the landlady.

In a hazy mist, I watch Simon sprint over to

her. And, a split second later, they vanish. He must be going for the cellar taking Doris with him. Clever boy! Just then, the pub door hits the wall and Sinjin Fury strolls in.

'Izzy!' he bellows. 'My best student ever. How wonderful to see you.'

Gritting my teeth, I get to my feet. 'Hello, Master,' I reply.

J A P A N

6th October, 1227 A.D.

'Today is Unarmed Combat Day.' Rubbing his hands, Fury shows me an alarming number of ivory teeth. 'We will begin with togadure-ryu.'

Instinctively, I clench my jaw. My third day of ninja school and I'm back in the temple, in the Rimankya Room. I slept deeply, no doubt my body's still recovering from yesterday's lessons, though, astonishingly, the welt on my finger vanished overnight.

The sorcerer steps up to me. No matter how

much he hurts me, I must not show it.

'The most important tool in the Seeker's or ninja's toolbag is not the sword, the blowpipe or the bow. It is the element of surprise.' Only a foot in front of him, I nod warily. Whatever togadure-ryu is, it's going to hurt.

Suddenly, his hands fly up and he claps me hard on the ears.

Bells ring and I cry out in agony. With a whimper, I drop to my knees.

'So you see, Izzy,' I can tell he is shouting but I only just catch his words, 'this particular method of disabling the enemy can be very successful.'

'No,' I mumble scornfully. 'Honestly?' My skull feels as if it's been split open with a blunt hatchet.

Bobbing down in front of me, he rubs my shoulder. 'I, of course, only hit you very, very gently.'

With a pathetic, almost babyish whimper, I topple over, thudding to the floor. There, I roll up in a ball and begin to weep.

'A drink, Felix,' Fury hops to his feet, 'till Izzy recovers. Then, when she feels up to it, I will hit her a little harder.'

Chapter 3

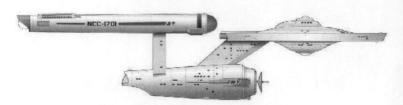

BUCKET O' BLOOD

With a sort of cowboy-swagger, Sinjin Fury struts over to me, a ginger cat scampering at his heels. I try to back away but there's nowhere to go and soon the sorcerer is standing over me, his lips snarled up in a victory snarl. 'Izzy, Izzy, Izzy,' he rasps, bowing sloppily. His English is almost perfect with just a tiny hint of a slur. 'Still trying to stop me, I see.'

I eye him coldly. I spot the silver buttons on

66

his tunic look old and patchy and there's a torn patch on his elbow.

Suddenly, he grips my chin in his fingers, his tomb-like eyes narrowing to slits. 'You remind me so much of your mother,' he says softly.

'You killed my mother,' I boldly hiss back, smacking his hand away. 'And if she was here, she'd try to stop you too.'

He steps away and nods lazily. 'Possibly,' he admits, swirling his umbrella.

He strolls over to a Glumsnapper sprawled on the floor. 'Good work, Izzy,' he says, poking the insensible monster with the tip of his boot. 'But, if I remember correctly, you always did do well in a fight.'

My stomach churns and I clench my fists. Very, very slowly, I feel for the hilt of my...

Suddenly, the cat begins to grow bigger and bigger, dropping fur and morphing into a skinny boy with spots. It is Fury's annoying little helper, Felix.

'Watch it!' Felix calls out. 'She's going for her wand.'

'What!? Oh, yes.' Fury snaps his fingers and my hand burns. I yelp as my wand jumps from my pocket and into his fist. 'Elm,' he murmurs, studying it, 'with a silver tip. Is this Cody's? Is the old drunk here? I do hope so. I'd very much enjoy killing him.' He stuffs it in his belt next to a jewel-barreled musket.

I turn and glower at Felix. 'Didn't I recently hex you?' I ask him, mockingly.

The wiry-thin boy scowls. 'I been pooping slugs for weeks.'

'How odd,' I reply, feeling wonderfully spiteful. 'A slug pooping slugs.'

The boy pulls his wand and steps up to me. 'Let's see if you enjoy it? But let's try a prickly cactus.'

'Now, now, kids,' Fury flicks his umbrella and the boy jumps back with a yelp.

'But,' protests Felix, 'she...' With a low growl, Fury turns on him and he stops. 'OK, OK.' He shrugs. 'Look, I did everything you asked. I told you she'd be here and here she is, And, if she's here, the boy's here too.'

'But where is he? All I see is this foolish girl.'

'My job was to find Izzy,' the boy persists. 'Just Izzy. We shook on it, remember?'

'So we did.' The wizard nods and pulls a bottle from his tunic pocket. 'Here's your reward, Boy.'

Unstopping it with his teeth, Fury drips three drops of red goo on Felix's lips. The boy licks them off then, shutting his eyes, he swallows. With a husky cry, he folds to his knees. He rests there, swaying back and forth, clutching his tummy. Then, suddenly, his chin snaps up, his jaws fly open and he howls.

I don't know what to do. Help him? Let him suffer? He's my enemy but, still, he's not always been. I step up to him. 'Felix, I don't know how to...' Suddenly, thankfully, he stops and shakily clambers to his feet.

'Be off with y',' says Fury, He idly taps the barrel of the musket on his belt. 'But, remember, if I call, be here. Understood?'

The boy nods and, with shaky steps, he reels drunkenly over to the door. Gloomily, I watch him go. 'Why?' I yell after him. 'You were a Seeker. The Sorcerers' Covern trusted you. I trusted you.'

He stops and slowly turns to look at me. 'I work for Lord Fury now. The pay's better.' Gritting his teeth, he yanks open the door and staggers out.

The seconds 'Tick, Tock' by in my mind. I can feel my blood pumping and my knees feel juddery and not at all up to the job of holding me up. Swaying a little, I twist and look at Fury, my old master. I must keep him talking until Simon sends help. If he can escape from the cellar, that is. 'What's in the bottle?' I ask him.

He grins horribly, displaying a jumbled row of rotten teeth. I remember, in Japan over eight hundred years ago, how ivory-white his smile had been. But dark magic, I know, rots the gums. 'Blood,' he says simply.

I scowl. Felix is scum but is he now a blood-sucking vampire too, I wonder.

'No, he's not,' says Fury.

'Stop it!' I hiss. I try to focus on a happy memory; it is the only way I know to shut my mind off to him. I think he finds happiness – my happiness anyway – uncomfortable. 'Why blood?' I snap.

His lips curl up and I think, for a second, he's not going to tell me. I feel his eyes travelling over me, studying me, sizing me up. Suddenly, I feel horribly dirty and in need of a shower and a good scrub. Then he shrugs. 'Deep under Bucket O' Blood Cemetery, the blood of the entombed collects.'

'The blood of wizards,' I murmur.

'Yes, yes.' He nods wildly. 'But most of them were of no interest to me. But for...' he stops and his eyebrows lift. 'Tell me Izzy, who, of all the wizards in this century, was the most powerful? Who is lying there in the dirt?'

I think for a second. Then it hits me and I swallow. 'Glumweedy.'

'Yes, Fester Glumweedy. A fool but a very clever fool. His blood was hidden deep in the rock under the cemetery and difficult to find. But it did not matter and I started to drill. Day and night until, finally, I was rewarded. Then I drank my fill.'

I swallow. The power of Glumweedy now rests in Fury. He must be stopped. But how? 'And Felix? Why did he drink the blood?'

'He's a follower so, when he helps me, he's rewarded. But just a drop or two. Glumweedy's power needs to be here,' he thumps his chest, 'in me. I don't need a revolt on my hands.'

I step boldly up to him. 'But why?'

With a snigger, Fury rubs a bony thumb over the musket on his belt. 'Greed,' he says simply. 'A rich man wants only to be richer. Yes, my magic is powerful but, with Glumweedy's blood in me, I can do anything. Be EVERYTHING! And, so long as I possess it, my army of monsters will never defy me. They flock to me now, keen to drink my brew. I return them to power and they, in turn, destroy what I order them to destroy. And, now, they will kill any Seeker I tell them to.'

'And Simon?'

'He'll be the jewel in my crown, Think of it,

74

Izzy...'

'Don't call me...'

'THINK OF IT!' he yells. Sparks fly from the tip of his umbrella and, with a whimper, I stumble back. Suddenly, he words soften, 'To kill with a wish. I'll be invincible.'

'But who do you wish to kill?' I persist. 'Ogun? But Simon's power will not work on a sorcerer – or a witch.'

For a second, he looks at me, his eyes cold and impenetrable. 'Do you honestly not know?'

I frown. 'No,' I say slowly, 'I honestly don't.' There is a secret there – a BIG secret – but I know he will not tell me. I know him too well.

'I do not wish to kill you,' he says at last. 'You were my best student. Why not work with me, Izzy? Then I will tell you everything.'

'Never. Ogun, with the help of the Sorcerer's Covern, will destroy you.'

'HA!' Fury scoffs. 'Ogun's a fool. He and his meddling sorcerers will bow to me. Everybody will bow to me.'

'I won't,' I hiss.

He nods slowly. 'I think a lesson is needed. Yes, a lesson to show you how powerful I truly am. Then you will understand the futility of trying to stop me.'

He lifts his umbrella and levels it at me.

I stiffen my knees and boldly glower up at him. If this is it, this is it. I'm not going to cower to this madman.

KAPOW!

A bomb seems to blow up in my skull...

CUTTING

SPLICING

RIPPING AT MY MIND!

With a yell of agony, I drop to my knees, clawing at my eyelids. 'Stop this!' I cry. 'STOP!'

'Whatever you say,' he jeers.

Instantly, the throbbing lessens as if I just swallowed the world's most powerful Aspirin. Slowly, I lower my hands. My jaw drops to my chin and my stomach turn to jelly. To my utter astonishment, I'm on a ship. And, I think...

OH NO! IT IS...

The ship is sinking!

Chapter 4

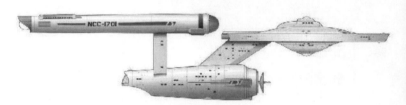

TINY FINGERS

A uniformed man in a puffed-up yellow vest elbows by me, knocking me to the deck. For a split second, he falters, then terror balloons in his eyes and he sprints off. 'Sorry, Miss,' he calls belatedly over his shoulder.

I clamber to my feet. 'Moron,' I mutter, nursing a cut on my hand.

I see I'm no longer in my Seeker uniform. Now, I'm dressed in a long, flowery gown and, under it – I peek – FRILLY BLOOMERS! A bonnet crowns my curls and flimsy slippers cover my feet. I prod my top lip with my tongue and taste lipstick.

The tilting deck is slowly flooding, the water swirling over my slippers. Gingerly, I drag my feet up the ship and away from the rising water. A tall, white funnel looms over me, lit up by the moon and, in a corner, a tiny orchestra of violins and a forlorn-looking cellist play a cheerful melody.

Most of the passengers milling the deck look dazed; I know that look. I remember seeing it in the mirror the day my mum and dad were killed. They think the alarm clock will soon ring and they will sit up in bed and stretch. They need to be told what to do but nobody, it seems, wants the job.

Peering over a metal banister, I discover I'm on a colossal ship and almost half of it is under water. A rocket zooms up into the night sky, exposing a lifeboat full of weeping children and silent mums. Wheels crank and men grunt as it is lowered down to the glassy water.

'Put this on, lass,' another uniformed man stuffs a vest in my hands, 'and get to safety.'

Instantly, I grip the hem of his jacket. 'What ship is this?' I bark. 'Where am I?'

But he's in too much of a hurry. Pulling free, he jogs off, flinging vests to the rest of the frightened passengers.

Wrestling to put it on, I spot a word embossed on the front and I get the biggest shock of my life. I suddenly find it very difficult to focus my eyes. I drop to my knees, the word embedded in my mind.

TITANIC!

Why did Fury send me here? And how did he do it? Is Glumweedy's blood so powerful? Did he not need the Cronus Mirror? Suddenly, my other problems seem unimportant; even Simon is driven from my mind.

I feel myself slipping. The ship is slowly keeling over, whimpering in her agony. Urgently, I jump to my feet and grip hold of the banister. I must keep dry for as long as I can. If this IS the Titanic then, I remember from my history books, the water is icy cold.

Further up the deck and, thankfully, away

from the rising water, I spot a portly man in a top hat and with curly whiskers. Hand over hand. I struggle over to him. 'I need help,' I pant. 'I must get off this ship.'

The man chews off the tip of a cigar and spits it out. 'Cuban,' he informs me, patting his pockets. 'Cost me twenty shillings. Can I possibly bother you for a light?'

'Em, no. Sorry.' I scowl at him. 'You do know this ship is sinking?'

'Yes, my girl, I do. Anyway, I'm Lord Cavendish-Brown.' He bows stiffly. 'You know, I do enjoy a good cigar but, it seems, I left my lighter in the cabin. Awfully annoying. I must send my man to fetch it. Now, where is the fellow? He's always slacking.'

I look at him in bewilderment. He's bonkers!

Pulling off my vest, I stuff it in the man's hands. 'Put it on,' I order him. 'I think it knots at the front.' Then, throwing off the silly bonnet and slippers, I stumble away.

I must find a way off this doomed ship. But how? Where do I go? I rub my hands briskly together. It's so cold and, here I am, dressed for a July night in the Sahara Desert.

The high-pitched screech of twisting metal rings in my skull and I look up to the see the funnel slowly toppling over. 'LOOK OUT!' I howl to a bonneted lady up to her knees in swirling water. A split second later, the hunk of metal lands in the water with a splash, crushing her.

Unblinking, I look on in horror, my feet rooted to the deck of the ship.

Over to my left, there is a yelling crowd of

Billy Bob Buttons

passengers who seem to be trying to get off the Titanic too. But a tall man in a uniform, holding a pistol, is keeping them back. 'Children first,' he hollers.

Excellent, I think. I'm 'children'.

Sprinting over, I begin to jostle my way through the angry mob. A lady in a red ball gown steps on my foot and a chunky man with a monocle elbows me in the eye. But I keep on going, pushing and shoving, forcing my way to the front.

At last, I get there, but the last of the lifeboats is already being lowered.

'But there's still room,' I holler indignantly at the man.

With a hardening jaw, he says nothing.

'Listen to me!' I screech, snatching at his

84

sleeve.

Like lightening, he lowers the pistol till the tip of the barrel is tickling the tip of my nose. 'Step away,' he commands me, his words shaking almost as much as the gun in his hand.

'Okay! Okay!' I whimper, hastily backpedaling and wishing I'd not left Cody's wand with Fury in the Crusty Crypt Inn.

The angry spark in his eye flickers out and, with a look of disgust, he casts the pistol away. 'Sorry,' he murmurs. 'Try over on the port side. You might be lucky.'

I nod. 'Thanks,' I say, turning away.

'But hurry,' he tells me, his hand pressing urgently into my back.

I trip and stumble my way over the slippery wood. Steeper and steeper, the Titanic tilts over so I must grip hold of iron ladders and the corners of doors to prevent myself from hurtling off the ship. Everywhere, men helter-skelter over the lopsided deck, yelping in panic and crying for help.

Scrambling over a fallen mast, I finally get to the port side of the ship. But, to my horror, all I find there is a metal winch and a dangling rope.

Urgently, I turn to a bedraggled crowd of passengers clinging to the winch. 'Where did all the lifeboats go?' I yell.

They ignore me but for a scruffily-dressed woman who is perched on the top of the banister. 'They left us,' she whimpers, looking at me beseechingly. 'The posh lot left us here to drown.' She pulls her legs up and over the top bar.

'No!' I holler, running towards her. But I'm too late and she jumps, her cry filling the bitterly cold night.

A deep, low growl erupts in the belly of the ship and the lights blink off. I stand there, just – stand there, only a tiny whimper invading my terror. The twinkling stars help me to spot a tiny boy; he is sitting, his knees up to his chin, under a ladder. I rush over and kneel down next to him.

'Where's your mummy?' I softly ask him. I see that his hand is shaking. On impulse, I cover it in my own.

'I lost her,' he snivels, his words trembling. He has on stripy pjs and boots on his feet; he looks to be seven or so. 'Can you help me to find her?'

I nod, squeezing his hand. 'Soon,' I promise him. 'If I can.'

The ship is almost vertical now, only the ladder welded to the wall preventing the boy and I from sliding away. Soon, I know, the rest of the ship will be under water and we will be thrown to the mercy of the freezing Atlantic.

Only seconds to go.

I remember the boy wedged in next to me. 'I'm Isabella,' I tell him.

'H-H-Henry,' he stutters back.

'So,' I frown, trying to think of things to say; difficult to do when sitting on the sinking Titanic, 'what do you do for fun? Play football? Watch TV?'

'What's a TV?' the boy asks.

'Oh, yes. Sorry.' I muster a grin; I forgot it's 1912 and TV's not been invented yet. 'Don't worry, when you get to sixty...' I stop, the rest of my words jammed in my larynx. Any second now, Henry's going to drown. No TV for him...

Then...

The swirling water hits me, surging up and over my body and filling my nostrils. It is agony, like hundreds and hundreds of tiny pins jabbing at my skin. Grimly, I hold onto Henry's hand and I feel his tiny fingers squeezing me back.

He must be so frightened. But there's nothing I can do to help him and, for the first time in my life, I feel totally and utterly powerless.

As I slowly drown in the icy waters of the Atlantic, a terrific hatred suddenly erupts up within me. Hatred for Fury; that he will now find Simon and there's nobody to stop him. Hatred for Rufus and the other Seekers for being so shifty and difficult and not properly helping me.

But, most of all, hatred for my mum and dad; if only they'd escaped the fire...

All of a sudden, I feel my body being yanked upwards as if I'm hooked on a fishing line, and I feel the boy's tiny fingers slipping from my grasp. A split second later, oxygen fills my bursting lungs and a velvety warmth smothers my skin.

Slowly, I lift my eyelids, half expecting to be sitting on a fluffy cloud, tiny angel wings fluttering on my back. But, to my jaw-dropping astonishment, I SEEM to be standing in a big, green tent!

'Well, this is much better,' I mutter.

Chapter 5

BULLY TINS AND
BARBED WIRE

'Relax trooper. Grab a pew. Drop of rum?
No? Good boy. You troopers drink too
much anyway. Wonderful news! We go
over the top at dawn.' The curly-moustached
man sitting on the stool in front of me titters.
'When I say 'we', not me. You! You and your men.
Lucky blighters! I must stay here; plan the next
skirmish. I volunteered you by the way. Your

regiment gets to fly the flag for England.' He flaps a hand at me. 'No, no, don't thank me. Now, have a butchers at this map. The Hun's here, dug in on the hill; they been up there for months. The only way to get to them is a full on attack. Sappers been tunneling for months. They plan to stick a bomb under the German trench and blow it up. Then, over you go. Willy Biggins will be on your flank. Excellent fellow. I play cricket with his dad. Well, I did. He lost his leg to a cannon ball. We plan to shell the blighters good and proper too. They'll be in shock by the time you get to them. They'll probably surrender or run off. A stroll in the park for your lads.'

I look blankly at him. Is he talking to me?

I'm standing in a green, canvas tent. The old fellow sitting at the desk in front of me is in a uniform and so, it seems, am I. My feet feel cramped in tall, black boots and my skin is itchy under my woolly tunic. I'm still pretty cold but thankfully not as cold as when I was drowning in the freezing Atlantic. I have on a metal helmet and a rifle is slung over my shoulder.

I flex my fingers. Only a second ago I'd been holding Henry's tiny hand. Poor kid. I hope he survived.

'Chat to your men, check gasmasks and bayonets. Bacon and jam for every fellow when they get back; and a day's rest too. Keep low and watch for snipers. How's the trench foot?'

'Em...'

'That bad, is it? Try a drop of whale oil. That'll do the trick. Ok, that's all, Trooper. Chop! Chop! Remember, if successful, the Battle of the

Somme will end the war.'

I look to my feet, wondering what trench foot is. He keeps calling me Trooper but can he not see I'm a teenage girl? I'm not even in the scouts.

He throws me a salute and I sort of wave feebly back.

Stumbling from the tent, I'm met by a gangly man caked collar to boots in mud. 'What did he say, Sir? We going over?'

'Yes,' I reply. 'I, er – think so. I lift off my helmet. 'At dawn.'

The man's shoulders droop. 'Then we'd better get back and tell the lads the good news.'

I nod.

Hunched over, he sets off. 'Sir,' he calls, not bothering to look back, 'better pop your tin potty on. Lots of snipers.'

Shoving my helmet back on, I reluctantly follow him.

The night is pitch black, the moon having run away in disgust; and it is snowing in big, fat lumps. There is a sudden flash of light followed by a boom and, suddenly, the sky is lit up for a second showing me a barren wilderness of muddy hills and burnt trees. A pony staggers by dragging a wagon. To my horror, I see it is jammed full of injured men crying and whimpering.

I'm in a world of rattling guns, whiz-bangs and barbed wire.

Trudging on, I keep my hands hidden in my deep pockets. Hanging over my shoulder, the rifle keeps nudging me, reminding me of where

Fury has sent me.

To war!

But how did he do it, I wonder. The only way I know of to send a person into history is using the Cronus Mirror. It is how Seekers hunt history for children of Ammit. But the mirror is in Gullfoss and protected by the Sorcerers' Covern.

'Is that you, Spink?'

'No, it's bleedin' Santa. Lower y rifle, dimwit.' Following Spink, I clamber down into a deep trench. 'Open y' lugs, lads,' Spink yells. 'Sir here, has a wonderful job for us.'

There must be fifty men in the trench. Swimming in mud, they sit there scoffing lumps of grisly-looking beef from battered tin trays; bully tins if I remember correctly.

96

Forks clatter to a stop and they all look at me expectantly.

'Is it true, Sir?' a young-looking trooper pips up, his eyes scared and bloodshot.

I look at him. How old? Sixteen? Seventeen? A few years older than me. 'Yes,' I reluctantly say. 'At dawn. After we shell them and the Sappers blow up the German trench.'

'The General says it'll be a 'stroll in the park',' offers up Spink. He must have been listening at the tent flap.

My lips suddenly feel terribly dry. I remember studying the Battle of the Somme in History. It had been a bloodbath. But I nod anyway.

Many of the men grin but I spot Spink looks much less cheerful at the prospect of attacking the Germans. I suspect he knows the terrible truth too.

Spink elbows the man sitting next to him. 'What did y' get?'

'Sweets,' he pops a yellow blob in his mouth, 'and a letter from my dad.' He looks up at me. 'Can you tell me what it says, Sir? Never been much good with words. A bit fiddly, I find.'

I nod. Moving over to stand next to a lantern, I unfold the damp paper.

Hello Jacob my boy,

Your mum and I hope this letter finds you well and in good spirits. She sends her love and told me to tell you she prays for you and your regiment every Sunday in church. Every day, the newspapers tell how gallantly the British army is fighting. It seems the Germans will surrender any day now and the war will finally be over.

The men in the trench guffaw at this. 'If only they knew,' mutters Jacob dejectedly.

Yesterday, I chatted to Mr Crunch, your old boss over at the wood mill. He told me there's plenty of work so, when you return, there's a job for you. Oh, and the roof on the chicken hut needs fixing too but I will hold off doing it until you can help me.

Now for the bad news. Your old football chum, Billy Potts, got hit in the eyes by shrapnel. Sadly, he's blind now but back with his family. I met his dad in the pub and he told me his son's not doing too well. When you get back you must visit him and try to cheer him up.

Cathy is dating a doctor from St Crispin's Hospital. She's very keen and we hardly ever seem to see her. Oh, and Granny's dog got shot by a farmer.

Enjoy the lemon bonbons and, by the way, your mum is knitting socks for you. Will send shortly.

Thinking of you, Dad

'Who's Cathy?' I ask, gently folding up the letter and passing it back to him.

'My sister.' Jacob slips it into his tunic pocket. 'Poor Billy, good lad, played keeper for The King's Arms.' He grins. 'Let in so many balls we all thought he was blind anyway.' He turns to Spink. 'What did you get?'

'A letter from my mum,' says Spink, wiping

down his bayonet with a rag, 'and my granny. My sister too. I think even the dog put paw to paper. But nobody sent me socks. My left foot's killing me.'

Trench foot. I remember Mum always told me to keep my feet dry and warm. I remember what the General in the tent told me too. 'Try whale oil,' I suggest.

Spink nods. 'I will. Cheers, Sir.'

'Y' not opening y' letters?' Jacob says to him.

'No.' He shrugs. 'When I get back.'

'But what if...'

Spink lobs a bully tin at him. 'If I'm killed, Granny's bad knees and my sister Sally's antics in the hayloft will be of no interest to me. But if I'm not, I can enjoy all the gossip over a bacon roll and a pot of jam.'

I perch on a rusty petrol drum and idly listen to the chatter of the men. Why did Fury send me here? To France? To a muddy trench in World War One. Being a Seeker, I often must travel in history, hunting for the children of Ammit. But never at the whim of a crazy sorcerer. Reluctantly, I look at my watch. Not long now. It's been a long night, sitting here, checking off the hours till dawn. Mostly, the men let me be, content to sit and chat: food and the lack of it, woman and the lack of them. A Welsh fellow attempted to sing 'Oh, Danny Boy' but the British guns were making such a racket drumming the German trench, he'd given up. During the night, the General had dropped by to tell the men what a very important job they were going to do. It seems I'm a sort of officer too. The men call me

'Sir' and look to me for support so I try to look confident and say, 'Chin up' and 'Soon be over' every opportunity I get.

A thundering boom rocks the trench. Staggering, I fall to my knees, mud drenching my body. Spink helps me up.

'This is it,' he cheerfully tells me. 'The Sappers just blew up the German trench.'

In a daze, I nod. Panic is starting to creep over my body. I'm finding it difficult to swallow and my lips feel puffed up and dry. The men gather by the foot of the ladders. I stumble over to them. There's no words left in me but for a husky, 'Good luck' to the man praying by my elbow.

If Fury's watching, I hope he plans to whisk me away if a bullet has Isabella etched on it.

'Y-you too, Sir.' A stuttered reply, dripping with terror.

Hugging.

Handshaking.

Then, a whistle blows.

A grim-looking trooper clambers up the ladder. Clutching a rifle I don't know how to work, I clamber up after him.

Peering over the top, a labyrinth of muddy craters meets my eyes. I feel my knees almost buckle as mortars spit and guns clatter, 'YAK! YAK! YAK!'

A man below me on the ladder slaps my foot. 'Get going, Sir!'

Scrambling up the last two rungs of the ladder, I set off, but my boots trip over a body slumped in the mud and I tumble to my knees. It is Jacob, his eyes glassy and staring.

A hand grabs me by the belt and yanks me to my feet. 'Keep up,' says Spink. 'Bacon and jam when we get back.'

I nod, not comprehending a word.

We rush on, clattering guns spraying a lethal storm of metal at us. Everywhere, men fall in the mud. Spink falls too and I drop to my knees next to him.

Trembling, his tunic torn and bloody, he grabs for my hand. 'I wish I'd opened my letters,' he sputters. 'God, I miss my mum.'

I nod. 'Me too.'

'And my foot's still murdering me.' He titters, spilling blood on his chin.

Gritting my teeth, I clasp his fingers tightly. 'I'm going to get you the warmest woollen socks

I can find,' I tell him. 'The very best.'

I feel a hammer blow to my stomach and I keel over, my body covering Spink.

Over my limp form, the guns keep clattering away. They seem not to worry that all the troops have been killed.

Chapter 6

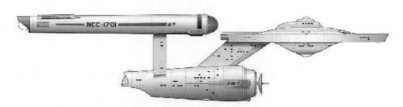

EVERYBODY THINKS
I'M A LUNATIC

'IZZY!' I jump up, knocking my elbow on the corner of a filing cabinet. 'Pop over to Sally's office, will you?' A chubby man hands me a sheet of paper. 'Oh, and tell her the meeting is now at ten thirty and not eleven.' He scowls at me. 'Chop! Chop! Soon be lunch.' Then he twists on his heels and lumbers off.

Nodding dumbly, I gently pat my stomach.

Then I peek down the front of my shirt. No blood; not even a tiny scar.

Looking up, I see I'm now in a modern-looking office. Everywhere, fingers tap plastic keys and coffee mugs sit on cluttered desks. A skinny man is photocopying and a flashing fax beeps and spills paper on the grey carpet.

I stand and listen for a second. From the accents, I think I must be in America.

I feel the knot in my stomach slowly unwind. Compared to being on the sinking Titanic or in a muddy trench, fighting Germans, this is much, MUCH safer. Unless a rogue stapler or a pencil sharper suddenly attacks me.

Now, what to do with this silly memo? I wander over to the lifts. Perhaps Sally's office is on a different floor.

So, up or down?

Up.

I press the button. A gold arrow over the doors twirls...

94, 95, 96

Wow! This tower is tall. It must be a skyscraper. The doors slither open with a 'PING!' but I don't step in. The most terrifying thought just hit me.

No.

No way!

No way Fury sent me there.

Dropping Sally's memo on the carpet, I dash over to the photocopy man. 'What day is it?' I bark at him.

He turns to look at me. Then he rubs his bristly chin. 'The 12th, I think.'

Thank God!

'No, no. Hold on.' He wags a finger at me. 'I took the bus up to Boston yesterday to see my old pops. It was his birthday. He turned 87 on the 10th, so today must be...'

My jaw sags. 'The 11th,' I mutter.

The man nods. 'Yep. The 11th of September.'

Oh no! I feel a shiver run up my spine, OH NO! I sprint over to the window and there, rising up from the city of New York, is a second silver tower. My Dad's sent me back to 2001, to the twin towers. And, any moment now, terrorists will fly jumbo jets into them, killing everybody.

I scan the sky but there's nothing to see. I

look over at a clock on the wall.

8.37

No help there. I can't even remember if it happened in the morning or the afternoon. Anyway, it's not important. My job now is to get everybody out. Including me!

'Izzy, did you find Sally and tell her?'

I twist on my heels to find the chubby man looking crossly at me.

'W-what?' I stammer.

'I told you to...'

'We must go.'

'No,' the man says slowly. 'YOU must go to Sally's...'

'WE MUST GO!' I snarl savagely.

With a frown, the man steps back. 'Izzy, I know it's a little hot in here but...'

Sprinting over to a desk, I jump up on it, knocking over a pot of pens, scattering them on the carpet. 'Listen to me,' I yell. 'Any second now, a passenger jet is going to hit this tower.'

A stony hush meets my words. Everybody in the room turns to look at me. Then, as if they all telepathically agreed I'm a total and utter lunatic, they go back to work.

'Get down off the desk, Izzy.' It is the photocopy man. 'I rang Security.'

But, over the top of his shiny skull, I just spotted a 'BLOB' moving in the sky. A bird?

A VERY, VERY BIG BIRD?

Jumping down, I elbow by the man and run

over to the window. 'Izzy,' he begs, scampering after me. 'This is crazy.' Ignoring him, I press my nose up to the glass.

'My God,' I murmur. Twisting on my heels, I grip the man's jumper. 'There it is,' I tell him. 'THERE IT IS!'

'Having a spot of bother, Tony?' A woman in a red cap walks over. Security!

Tony shrugs. 'Izzy here's acting a bit - odd.'

'No, I'm not!' I seethe, I wave an emphatic hand at the window. 'Look! You see there. The plane. Well, any second now, it's going to hit this tower. We must get everybody out of here. We must,' I chew vehemently on my lower lip, trying to think, 'I know! Set off the fire alarm.'

The woman frowns at me. Then she lifts her chin and sniffs. 'I can't smell any smoke,' she says.

This is getting me nowhere. With a growl, I rush back over to the lifts. I remember seeing...

Yes! There! By the silvery doors, a red box on the wall.

In the Event of Fire

Smash the Glass

I lift my fist but a hand grabs it, pulling me away.

'Get off me!' I cry.

'Now, now, try to relax...'

'Er, Lucy,' Tony prods the woman in the ribs, 'that jet is flying very low.'

I feel her hand loosen. Twisting to look too, I feel my knees turn to jelly.

TIME'S UP!

Then, suddenly, the floor shivers under my feet and the screech of twisting metal rings in my skull. For a split second, I feel the skin on my cheeks melt and my eyebrows burn. Then, a frosty wind blows over me and, slowly, I drag open my eyes.

I'm back in the Crusty Crypt Inn – AND in my Seeker dress – Fury, my tormentor, standing in front of me.

A pitiless whisper drills into my mind. *'Enjoy the history lesson?'* the sorcerer scoffs me.

'But – WHY?' I snarl.

'Ships sink, men kill men, terrorists hijack passenger jets. Nobody can stop it happening so why bother to try.'

'I don't understand.'

'My destiny, Izzy, is written in the stars. You will not stop me, you CANNOT stop me, so – why – bother – to – try!'

'You think so, do you?' I storm back at him.

'I know so.' He prods me with his umbrella. 'Now, stop this silliness and work for me, or I will show no mercy.'

I begin to rock on my heels, my eyelids fluttering. I can feel the anger welling up in me, flooding me belly like hot, bubbling acid. He put me through all of this just to show me how powerful he is and how helpless I am? I clench

116

and unclench my fists. I can still feel Henry's tiny fingers in my hand. I can still smell Spink's blood. With a wild cry, I slap the umbrella away. 'On December 25th, 1227, I told you my answer. I will never bow to evil,' I hiss.

He eyes me coldly. 'Yes, I remember. Pity,' Then he pulls Cody's wand from his belt and hands it to me. 'Then let's finish this,' he says. 'Here and now.'

J A P A N

27th October, 1227 A.D.

'This here is Hattori.' Fury wheels over a wooden dummy from the corner of the room. I must say it looks very human: quartz-rock eyes, mopish curls, even a bristly moustache and a mole on the cheek. 'Named after the legendary ninja, Hattori Hanzo,' he tells me, 'of the 17th century.'

I nod. Being a Seeker, Fury is allowed to travel to and fro in history and I wonder if he's ever met this legendary killer who's not even been born yet.

'Today we will be working with the fist, the foot and the knee. Let's begin with the fist.' He looks over to my keeper. 'Felix, if you will kindly show Izzy here how to do it.'

The weedy-looking boy skips over and, without a moment's thought, thumps the mannequin. My chin drops to my collar bone and wide-eyed, I study what's left of poor Hattori's ribs.

'Gotta hurt,' I mumble.

'Tremendous job, Felix.' Smirking, the boy swells up his sparrow chest and scampers off back to his sentry post by the door. Then Fury looks to me. 'He's a Seeker too and very talented.'

'Hmm,' I nod mockingly. 'Amazing for such a wimp.'

His jaw hardens and I spot the tiny, almost imperceptible twitch of his left cheek, but he lets it go. 'Now then, Izzy, your turn. Hattori's torso is a little er, destroyed, so hit him on the chin. Hard.'

Gritting my teeth, I curl up my hand and thump it, almost shattering my knuckle. With lewd words spurting from my lips, I nurse my fingers in my armpit.

'No, Izzy,' he barks, a dangerous spark in his eye. 'He's your enemy, not your sixty-three-year-old grandmother. I told you to hit him hard. HARD!'

He knows my grandmother's sixty-three!

My eye sparks too but, dutifully, I follow his order.

Fury rolls his eyes and tuts. 'No, no, NO! You

must pretend Hattori here is trying to murder you; not just you, your family too,' his eyes narrow evilly, 'even your poor mother, Kitta, and your father, Hickory. Such a tragedy.'

My top lip flips up in a snarl. He knows way too much. WAY TOO MUCH! And I very much want to wipe the sneer off his face

But I still my temper. I keep my wits and with a blood-curdling growl I turn my anger on the dummy.

'Now hit him hard,' Fury instructs me. 'Pretend he's the man who lit the match and burnt your parents.'

THUD! THUD! THUD! THUD! THUD!

'Good, Izzy. Good. You will be a Seeker in no time.' He bows. 'I will pop back soon to check on your progress.'

Two agonisingly long hours later, he dutifully returns, but by then my fist is a blood-spattered pulp and my mood is volcanic.

He looks to the dummy and his eyes narrow. 'Excellent,' he murmurs. 'Excellent! I see Hattori's chin is very slightly dented.'

I roll my eyes. I very much doubt it is. The dummy's chin is rock hard and all I can see is my blood all over it.

'Look!' The sorcerer knocks on the wood with his knuckle. 'I think you even splintered it.'

'Yes, well, I pretended he was you,' I say jokingly. Well, sort of jokingly.

He titters but I spot his hand shift a little closer to the sword on his belt. 'Whatever works for you, Izzy. Now, rest your fist,' I nod thankfully, 'and let's see how hard you can hit

Hattori with your knee and foot.'

I look to him in frank astonishment, my mouth doing a perfect impression of a fly trap. He must be crazy.

He claps me cheerfully on the shoulder. 'And then, I think, it will be time for you to jump over the pond.'

Chapter 7

DROOLING JAWS

All of a sudden, just to my left, there is a low growl. I jump, almost dropping Cody's wand. Then, slowly, I turn to look.

'Oh, sweet Jesus,' I mutter. For there, over by the pub's door, is a Dorfmoron.

A GIGANTIC DORFMORON!

Bigger than a bulldozer, he is covered from jaws to claws in a straggly, snowy-white pelt. Jagged teeth the size of elephant tusks erupt from a cave-like mouth and from the top of his

124

skull spring two horns, sharpened to icepicks.

A gasp of horror slips from my lips. With my knees buckling, I back away, my bum colliding with a stool, tipping it over.

'But – but, this is CRAZY,' I stammer. 'I can't fight him. He's bigger than a bus.' I turn to the sorcerer. 'I thought...'

'What?' says Fury scornfully. 'Did you think you and I were...HA! Don't be silly, child. My monsters do my dirty work, not me.'

'But – he'll murder me. Master, you can't let him.'

'Oh! So now I'm Master.'

'But I'm...'

'A pest. Yes,' he growls, 'I know.

The Dorfmoron snarls menacingly. He is pacing to and fro, clenching and unclenching his claws. I sprint over to the bar and duck down behind it. The trapdoor, I see, is still up. For a second, I'm tempted to scarper, but what if Simon didn't find a way out and he's still down there with Doris? Sinjin Fury and his Dorfmoron will follow me and find him. I can't let that happen. But what do I do? Will my spells even work on a monster with claws so big they'd rip a cow in half?

Do I stay...

Or do I run...

But the Dorfmoron picks for me. Suddenly, he rips up the bar, showering me in Cheesy Wotsits, and throws it across the pub. I jump to my feet. Now there's nothing standing in his way; nothing between me and a drooling jaw of teeth.

Slowly, he lumbers over to me.

'Now, let's not be hasty,' I whimper, wishing fervently I knew the Dorfmoron word for 'surrender'. But the monster's not in a prisoner-taking sort of mood and he kicks me so hard in the chest I'm almost knocked to my knees. I toss my lantern at him and lift my wand, but the monster's too fast, so fast I can no longer see his claws or feet, but I feel them, in my eye, my jaw, my poor knee.

With a howl, he jumps up, his foot hunting for my chin, but I block it and punch him in the belly. He staggers back, his bushy eyebrows arched. The big monster, I think, did not expect the tiny girl to show her teeth.

With fists flying, he clumps back over to me, but I duck, drop low and sweep my foot. Nimbly – for a big, furry monster anyway – he jumps over it. Not good! And now it's his turn.

He thumps me; an uppercut to the jaw. Then he twists and flips me over his shoulder, cartwheeling me to the floor. I clamber drunkenly to my feet. 'JELLYIFY!' I yell, the only spell I can think of. But, sadly, I miss. A hammering fist wallops me on the cleft of my chin, cracking my teeth. I lurch back, hitting the pub wall and dropping my wand. Blurry-eyed, I watch him march up to me, murder glinting in his pot lid-shaped eyes.

'MASTER, STOP HIM!' I cry. 'This is crazy.' But the monster is on me like a fat boy on a muffin.

Gripping me by the neck, the Dorfmoron slams me back up to the wall. I feel his sharp claws digging into my skin. I grab for his paw, trying to wrench it off, but he's stronger than

English mustard.

Suddenly, a rage fills me from my boots to the tops of my curls. I thrust up my chin, the monster's wiry fir scratching the tip of my nose. 'GET – OF – ME!' I wheeze.

The monster snarls back at me and, in that split second, I see my opening. Yanking a skull bomb off my belt, I twist the top and jam it between two of the monster's jagged teeth.

Instantly, he unclasps my neck and I drop ragdollishly to the floor. Seeing stars, I zigzag over to my fallen wand and cower there. A split second later,

BOOM!

Very, VERY slowly, I look up.

To my horror, the monster is still on his feet. But, still, I think the bomb injured him. He's swaying back and forth like a confused robot, bulldozing into the wall. Thankfully, with a whimper, he drops to the floor.

If I'm going to win this fight, now might be my only chance.

In a burst of wild fury, I snatch up my borrowed wand and march over to where the Dorfmoron now sits.

'Do it,' The words swirl in my skull. *'You know the spell.'*

I swallow. Yes, I do. The Killing Spell. Fury showed it to me in the Book of Spells when I was only ten. 'But – it is not the Seeker's way,' I stammer.

'But it IS my way. Do it. Then, together, we will find the boy and...'

'I'M NOT WTH YOU!' I cry. My knees crumple and, with a pathetic, almost babyish whimper, I fold to the floor. There I stay, my wand resting in my lap. I can't keep fighting him. I just can't. It's slowly killing me...

I watch the Dorfmoron crawl over to a corner of the pub. Fury balloons his cheeks and jumps off his stool. Then he strolls over to me. 'If my monster can't do, I will do it.' He stops and looks at me, his eyes overflowing with scorn. 'If only Kitta and Hickory had had a boy,' he says. Then, he lifts his wand...

Suddenly, the window shatters, glass and shards of wood spraying the pub. A split second later, Rufus is standing over me.

'Hello, Sinjin,' he says, helping me to my feet.

'Rufus, old fellow. How wonderful of you to drop in. Cody too, I see. Still on the sherry, yes? Excellent.' I look over to the door and see the tubby Seeker is there. He winks at me and taps his wand expectantly on his knee. 'My old student and I were just, er – catching up. I miss her terribly.'

'I bet,' mutters Rufus.

'So, tell me, where's the boy?'

'Boy?'

Fury smirks and twirls his umbrella. 'It's always the difficult way.' He looks over at the Dorfmoron. 'Get up Jumble Mud,' he spits. Reluctantly, the monster clambers to his feet. Then Fury turns back to the Seeker. 'Do you honestly think you and old Cody there can stop me? It's a joke.'

With a tiny twitch of his lips, Rufus steps up to him. I look on in astonishment; Rufus is a powerful Seeker but he's no match for Fury. But, here he is, facing up to him and I think he's even SMILING! 'Sinjin, this madness must stop. A son of Ammit is not a clockwork toy. You can't just wind him up and play with him. He must be sent to Gullfoss and his powers destroyed.'

'Do not lecture me, old man,' sneers Fury, sparks erupting from the tip of his umbrella. 'The Loki will do what I tell him to do. Now, where – is – he?'

Rufus sighs. 'So be it.' He lifts his wand. 'Go, Izzy. Get Simon to Ogun. He'll know what to do.'

I scowl. 'But I can't just...'

'GO!' he yells.

Fury snorts. 'Izzy's not going anywhere,' he says coldly. 'Oh, and Cody y' fool,' he turns to the Seeker who has now crept over to the window, 'I CAN SEE YOU!'

But I see my opening and sprint for the door. I must find Simon. Two steps. Three steps. Six to go... On my heels, the floor erupts in a flurry of splinters. A Lightning Spell. 'STOP!' Fury yells. But, with legs pumping, I keep on running.

BOOM!

The pub shudders. Pints of beer spill over and stools crash to the floor. Rufus and Cody must be firing spells, trying to cover my escape. But they don't know Fury's been drinking

Glumweedy's blood. They don't know how powerful he now is.

Almost there.

Almost...

With a howl, Jumble Mud jumps in my path. But not even a seven-foot monster can stop me now. At full pelt, I drop to my knees and slither between the Dorfmoron's stumpy legs. Then, I jump to my feet, kick open the door and stumble out into the thundery night.

JAPAN

9th November, 1227 A.D.

'The ability to keep perfectly still is the most important of the Seeker's skills,' Fury instructs me. 'You, Izzy, must be the tree on the windless day.'

I tut and stifle a yawn. To the sorcerer every Seeker skill is the most important skill.

'If you wish to successfully ambush your enemy,' my instructor chatters on, 'it is vital he not spot you. Remember, depend on surprise, not brute strength to win the day.'

I blink but do not nod. If I do, Felix will spot it.

DROWNING FISH

My job is to keep perfectly still for three hours and I'm determined to pass the test.

I'm stood on a barrel in the Rimankya Room. Fury and the boy sit on pillows in front of me, chopsticks working furiously on bowls of beef and rice.

I'm hungry too, starving in fact, and my stomach growls angrily at the insult.

This is my thirty-sixth day of ninja school and I'm utterly exhausted. Every hour of my seventeen-hour day is now crammed full of climbing unclimbable trees, jumping unjumpable ponds and listening jadedly to Fury's non-stop summary of ninja history. In truth, not so much a summary, but the unabridged works. True, I do feel strong, and I can run faster and jump higher than a deer in a pit full of tigers, but I'm still finding it terribly difficult to keep up.

My body is a disaster zone too, my elbows, my fists, even my knees and the bottoms of my feet cut to ribbons from pummelling poor Hattori. Mind you, my body will recover in a day or so. I don't know how and I don't know why, but it will. Thankfully, the dummy is in even worse shape than me and after almost two weeks of punching and kicking him, he is now a mere pile of matchsticks in the corner of the room.

'Time up, Izzy,' Fury claps his hands, 'you can stop now. Excellent work. You were most definitely the tree, though perhaps on a slightly breezy day.'

Deflated, my shoulders sink, a balloon the day after a birthday, and I clamber gingerly off the beer barrel. I feel horribly stiff, there is cramp in my legs and my stomach is howling furiously for food.

'So, what's on the menu, boys,' I joke, 'succulent pork ribs smothered in honey or, er - beef and rice?'

Fury hops to his feet. 'There'll be food shortly, Izzy, but first...'

He nods sharply to Felix, who, smirking callously, lumbers out of the room only to return a moment or two later lugging a second wooden dummy.

The boy plants it in front of me, his eyes cold and challenging.

'Allow me to introduce you to Hattori's brother,' Fury informs me coldly. 'Hijikata.'

A volcano erupts in my belly, red mist blurring my vision. Thirty-six days of physical punishment and tiny bowls of rice and I snap. Suddenly, I storm up to the dummy and in a five second blaze of elbows, feet and fists, I reduce it to splinters.

I look to my Seeker instructor, my eyes daring him to introduce me to any more of Hattori's chiselled family.

Fury's chin drops to his chest; he eyeballs me with the sort of puzzled interest a doctor shows when he sees a particularly nasty rash. Felix, however, looks positively sickened, as if I had just murdered his pet puppy. His eyelids twitch like a bull bothered by a fly.

'I'm famished,' I mutter, flexing my battered fingers.

Recovering his composure, Fury musters up a smile. 'Food it is,' his eyes narrow to tiny slots, 'or she might murder the cook.'

I nod. 'I probably will,' I tell him flatly, stomping off to the kitchen.

Chapter 8

THUNDER AND LIGHTNING
SPELLS

I run...

And I run...

And I run...

Thunder booms over Devil's Ash and icy droplets drum the streets and sandpaper my cheeks and chin. The storm is not so much over me, but EVERYWHERE and I'm drenched to the skin. But I do not slow down. I know Rufus and

Cody will not stop Fury; the sorcerer's too powerful for them and, soon, he will be on my heels.

The land judders and I stumble, almost tripping over a kid's bicycle. Reluctantly, I slither to a stop. The puddle by my feet begins to ripple and a tree drops conkers on the street. A Thunder Spell, I wonder, or simply the crushing footsteps of the Dorfmoron.

I stand perfectly still, my wand up, my eyes hunting the cold mist. I know Fury's out there, him and his monster, on the hunt for his prey. I can almost feel him.

'WHERE IS SHE!?' A yell from the fog.

Abruptly, the judders stop and, slowly, step by tiny step, I back away.

'Don't try to run, Izzy.' Fury's icy tenor plays

in my skull. *'Remember the lesson. You cannot stop me, so why bother to try.'*

With a gulp, I backpeddle faster...

And faster...

AND FASTER...

'Got you!'

I twirl so fast, I crick my neck. But, still, I'm too slow. With a terrifying growl, the Dorfmoron is on me. 'Rootify!' I bellow, but my Stopping Spell just ricochets off his thick pelt and I'm thrown brutally to my knees.

'Lord Fury,' he booms, 'I got her. She's over here.'

As if by magic – which it probably is – the mist lifts and I see my tormentor. He strolls over to me, his umbrella still in his claw, his silver-barrelled musket still hooked on his belt.

He seems to glow with danger like a stepped-on python.

'So, it's 'Lord' now, is it?' I scoff.

He looks to me, a sneer creeping over his pencil-thin lips. 'Good work, Jumble Mud,' he croons. He slaps the monster on the back and a puff of dust blooms up. 'OK, let's do this. Kill her for me.'

But the Dorfmoron stays stubbornly put. I think he just spotted the second Skull Bomb hooked to my dress. The monster's not so stupid after all.

'Must I do everything?' Fury growls. 'OK, OK. Just stay there and keep watch for Jagger Steel. If Cody's here – he's here.'

'Where is Cody?' I hiss. 'And Rufus? Did you hurt them?'

'Hurt them! No, no. I'd never JUST hurt them,' he says breezily. 'I sent them on a little trip. TO HELL! Now, GET – UP!'

I clamber drunkenly to my feet and stonily eyeball the sorcerer. But I see two – no, three of him; my eyes will not focus. Possibly from my brawl with Jumble Mud. That, or from my dip in the Atlantic. Or from being shot at by Nazis. OR FROM BEING HIT BY A PASSENGER JET!

Jadedly, I rub my cheeks. All in all, a pretty hectic day.

'Just the three steps, I think,' says Fury charitably. 'That knee looks a little, er – swollen up.'

I nod. He's right. And it hurts terribly. I remember Rufus telling me not to run on it but, it seems, I'm not a very good listener. 'Why?' I mutter, lifting my wand. 'Is Simon so important?'

The sorcerer titters, a mocking twinkle in his eye. 'The boy's not important,' he scoffs, 'but his power is. He's just a tool in my toolbox. He will bow to me, he will help me and then I will feed him to my Glumsnappers.'

My lips curl up in a snarl and I feel my eyes sharpen. With a grunt, I limp over to the Dorfmoron, thrust my hand up his left nostril and yank out a fistful of snot. Then I hitch up my dress and I rub it on my poorly knee.

Fury nods slowly. 'A Rufus trick.' He grunts. 'Clever girl.'

'Go to hell,' I reply with vigour.

He titters and bow to me. Stiffly, I mirror him. I do not wish to but it is the Seeker way. Then we stand back to back.

147

'One,' Fury growls.

So this is it.

'Two.'

Who will help Simon now? And who will stop Fury from finding him?

'Three.'

'FOR MUM AND DAD!' I cry. With red fury exploding in my chest, I twist on my heels and...

A rope thumps me in the chest and, unthinkingly, I grip it. Then...

...I'm whisked off my feet.

Up and up I go.

'COWARD!' bellows Fury, a Lightning Spell sizzling the heels of my boots. But he can't stop me now, I look back and, for a split second, I see the shimmer of rage in his eyes. Then, thankfully, his contorted face is lost in the mist.

'Ow!' I yelp. Urgently, I peer down to see Fury's Dorfmoron is clinging to the rope too. Growling and hissing, he is clawing wildly at my boots.

I scowl. How did he...?

Gritting my teeth, I thump the rope with the tip of my wand. I do not wish to kill this monster – he's just Fury's tool – but war's war and I know he'd happily kill me. 'DESOLATI!' I bellow, the spell almost lost to the howling wind. By my feet, the twisted strands slowly melt and the Dorfmoron plummets to his doom.

'Sorry,' I murmur.

Choking back vomit, I look up. But there's so much mist, I can't see where the rope ends. I suspect it must be hooked to the basket under the balloon Rufus, Cody and I travelled in from

Trotswood to Devil's Ash. But who's in it now, I wonder. Ally – or enemy?

Gritting my wand in my teeth, I begin the long climb. But the rope is old and bristly and cuts deep welts into my hands. Soon, it is slippery with my blood. But I keep on going. I must find Simon. If I don't, Fury's Glumsnappers will.

Finally, I see it. It IS the balloon we travelled in to Devil's Ash but I'm hanging directly under the basket so I can't see who's in it now. I chew on my lip, tasting blood. Whoever it is, they don't know I'm here. So, let's see if I can surprise them...

But, out of nowhere, two hands yank me off the rope and, like a sack of spuds, I'm tossed into the basket. For a second, I lay there, winded, nursing my bloody palms. Then, reluctantly, I look up...

'Steel!' I cry. I almost want hug him. Almost. And there, by his elbow, is Simon.

The burly Seeker helps me to my feet. 'Where's Rufus and Cody?' he asks me urgently.

'I – I don't know,' I reply, slipping my wand in my pocket. 'They took on Fury in the pub. Rufus ordered me to scarper, to find Simon, so I...'

'Left them there?'

Shifting my feet, I nod. 'Yes. I'm sorry. I didn't want to but...'

'There's blood on your hands,' Simon interrupts me.

I turn to him, wondering, for a second, if he's being metaphorical. 'Yes. Yes, I know.'

'If they get infected, your fingers will drop off.'

I guess he's not. 'They'll be ok,' I tell him, my lips twitching.

'It's not funny.'

'I know. Sorry.'

Steel stamps his foot. 'So, Rufus and Cody took on Fury, you say. I bet it didn't end well.'

'No, I don't think it did.'

The Seeker's eyes narrow. 'You didn't see?'

'No, I...'

'So there's a strong possibility they were only injured.'

'Not strong, no. I don't think Fury showed them much mercy. It's not his – way. His spells only ever seem to kill.'

Steel glowers mulishly at me. 'But, oddly, they never seem to kill you,' he says. Then, he pulls a lever and the balloon beings to drop. 'I still must try to find them. A Seeker never deserts a Seeker,' he turns and eyes me coldly, 'or did your Master not tell you that?'

I glare back at him, my jaw hardening. He knows Fury was my tutor; everybody knows and that's why nobody trusts me. But why bring it up now? 'Listen to me, Steel. There's no way Rufus and Cody overpowered Fury back in the Crusty Crypt.'

'Don't be ridiculous,' barks the Seeker with a harsh laugh. 'Rufus is a very...'

'He's been drinking Glumweedy's blood.'

Steel's chin drops to his chest. 'Fester Glumweedy? But, but – how? He's er...'

'In Bucket O' Blood Cemetery. Yes, I know. Fury dug him up. He's so powerful, he sent me to 1909 and he didn't need the help of the Cronus

Mirror to do it.'

'Bedbugs drink blood,' pips in Simon helpfully. 'But Fury's too big to be a bug. Or a tick. Ticks drink blood too.'

Steel looks at him in astonishment.

'Not now, Mop.' I step up to the other Seeker. Fury murdered Rufus and Cody. I know it – and you know it. We must accept it and find a way to...'

'But there's a possibility he didn't, so I must try.'

Stiff-jawed, he turns his back on me. I eye him with a scowl. Steel's no hero – not in my book, anyway. But, here he is, planning to dash off and face Fury. Why, I wonder. What's in it for him?

'When Rufus and Cody ran to the Crusty Crypt to help you, Rufus ordered me to stay and

DROWNING FISH

protect the boy.' Still talking, he keeps his back
to me. 'But now I don't need to. Now you can do
it.'

'But...'

'Seekers don't desert Seekers,' he insists.

I nod slowly. He's right. Still, he's deserting
ME. 'OK,' I say, 'but I'll go with you.'

'No. It's too risky. We must split up. Get the
boy to Gullfoss and I'll try to meet you there.'
Suddenly, he twists on his heels and steps up to
me. 'Don't let him in, Izzy.'

'Sorry?' My hand slips discreetly to the wand
in my pocket.

The Seeker rolls his eyes. 'Don't try to trick a
tricker, kid,' he says sternly. 'I know Fury's in
there.' He prods my skull. 'That's why I don't
trust you.' He snorts. 'And why no Seeker wants

to work with you.'

'Rufus trusts me,' I retort. 'He works with me.'

'But Rufus isn't here, is he. You left him in the pub, remember?'

'He told me...' I stop and swallow the rest of my words. He's just trying to get me cross.

The basket hits the dirt with a thump. Steel steps even closer and I get a whiff of strawberry from the gum he's been chewing. 'Don't listen to Fury's sly words,' he whispers. 'He's just playing with you. Don't let him in.'

I feel my jaw harden. This baboon thinks he knows me. AND he called me 'Kid'. My fist tightens on my wand. 'I'll try,' I say stiffly. If I hex him, he'll never trust me.

'Don't try. Do.' He offers me his hand. Reluctantly, I shake it, his grip too tight for my tiny fingers. Then he pulls his wand and jumps out of the basket.

So, it's up to me. I pull the lever and the balloon lifts off. And, if I don't do it, Fury will find Simon and kill anybody he wants. CLASSIC! I turn to the boy. 'Looks as if it's just you and me, Cowboy.'

'I'm not a...'

'I know. I know, it's just a – forget it.' I eye him for a second. His cheeks look a little yellow. 'Do you feel OK?'

He swallows then burps. 'All this up and down, up and down.' He holds his stomach. 'And it's so windy up here. I think – yes, yes, I am, I'm balloon sick.'

'Oh, er...'

'I'm sorry.'

'Don't be,' I tell him kindly.

'No, no, I'm sorry.' Then he bends over and throws up on my boots.

'Mop, honestly!' I sigh. Days just don't get any better than this.

J A P A N

22nd November, 1227 A.D.

Gritting my teeth, I squeeze the tip of my foot in a cranny and lever myself up the cliff. I'm almost sixty feet up Devil's Fork, a lump of rock a mile or so west of the temple. According to Fury, a Seeker must be able to climb a wall, a tree, even a cliff if he is to successfully hunt down a child of Ammit. Subsequently, I spent this week clambering up bamboo ladders and perfecting the art of the ippon sugi nobori, a clever tool for shimmying up tree trunks.

And now, finally, here I am, climbing a colossal chunk of rock.

For the first time ever, I'm in full Seeker garb, or shinobi shozoku in Japanese. It is a sort of tight-fitting cloth and is surprisingly robust. Unfortunately, I had not been allowed a rope and grapple for this climb, only shuko, a row of metal studs on the palms of my hands and the typical ninja split toe boot to help me grip with my feet.

My test for today is to climb the hundred and fifty feet to the top. The rock is in the shape of a three-pronged fork; I'm climbing the middle prong, Fury and Felix climb the outer two.

It is a race of sorts, a second bowl of beef and rice for the winner. I snort. Now, if it had been toffee pudding.

How I miss desserts.

DROWNING FISH

Fury, I see, is almost to the top of his. Blimey! The man climbs like a scalded monkey. The boy, however, is below me, and if I keep up my speed I know I can win our private little battle. I cannot resist a tiny smirk. He will be terribly upset.

As my eyes hunt the cliff face for a hold, I wonder to myself why he detests me so much. I know he's a Seeker, his job to assist Fury. But why's he not with the rest of the Seekers hunting for Ammit's children?

'HELP ME!'

I look over my shoulder to see the boy dangling by his finger tips from a tiny outcrop of rock. If he falls he will be killed.

'FELIX!' I yell. 'Try to put your foot up on the ledge.'

'I can't,' he yells back, his words drenched in

terror. 'My calf's cramped up.'

It must be a fifty foot drop to the rocks below. I must get to him; Fury, I know, is too far away to help.

'Just hold on!' I cry.

I bend my knees and with a roar I jump the six feet over to Felix's pinnacle of rock. I hit the cliff so hard I almost bounce off, my fingers frantically hunting the walls for a tiny cranny or a stump of rock to grip on to.

Fiercely, I hug the cliff wall. Why do I risk my life for this numbskull, I wonder. But I know why. To let him drop after he calls for my help would be cowardly. I enjoy the challenge of being schooled by Fury but I'm still repulsed by the Seeker's lack of morality. I do not wish to sink so low.

I loosen my hold and drop nimbly to the outcrop of rock only to discover Felix on his feet next to me.

'Surprise! Surprise!'

'Oh, y' safe. Good.' But I'm annoyed. I'd just risked my life to try to help him.

I expect him to scoff but he almost blinds me with a sunny smile. My eyebrows climb my brow; I'm shocked he knows how to, that he even has teeth. It is a warning sign, a fog horn, a flashing red light, but I miss it. I'm too slow.

He pulls his sword then swings it, slicing my cheek from eye to lip. Then he kicks me brutally in the kidneys and I reel back. My feet slip from the rock and I plummet, the studs on my clawing fingers catching on the lip of the rocky outcrop.

I hang there, a fish on a fish hook soon to be

'You called for help,' I cry to his boots. 'I was trying to save you.'

'Yes, I know. This need to be the hero is your undoing.' He looks coldly down on me, his eyes bold and pitiless, unmoving to my pleas as a tombstone.

'This is crazy,' I hiss. 'Why bother to enrol me in your ninja school if you just intend to murder me?'

He looks up, no doubt to check his master cannot see him. 'It is Fury and the Sorcerers' Covern, not I, who wish you to be here.' The words drip bitterly off his lips. 'Fury sees only you now. He thinks you will follow him but I know you cannot be trusted. It is my sworn duty to stop you.'

'But...'

'No, Izzy. No buts. But let me tell you this. Your mum and dad were killed in a fire, yes? Did you ever wondered who started it? Who lit the match? It was the man who saved you.'

'What?'

'IT WAS FURY!'

'No. NO!' I try to swing up my foot but he kicks it maliciously away.

'Now, let's see if you can fly.'

My fingers crunch under the heel of his foot and my hold is lost.

I plummet silently to the rocks below.

TODAY

Chapter 9

TRUTHS

Elbow to elbow, Simon and I watch the world drift slowly by. It is morning now and the sun is well up in the sky seemingly keen to show off Scotland's rolling hills, tiny woods and snaking rivers. It is so inspiring, I almost forget I'm on the run from a power-hungry wizard who seems very, VERY keen on killing me.

Like the balloon, my mind begins to drift too, to my 10th birthday when Dad told me he was a Seeker.

'A Seeker!' I'd responded in wonder.

I remember Dad nodded. 'A sorcerer,' he'd then whispered, 'who hunts history for the children of Ammit.'

'Who?' I'd asked.

'Ammit is a demon of the underworld, a destroyer and a hunter of men. When her children grew up they had children too. And so on and son on. A Seeker's job is to hunt history trying to find them. Trying to stop them. You see, Izzy, a child of Ammit can kill with just a tiny wish.'

'They must be terribly evil,' I'd whispered in horror.

'Yes. And no. We call them Loki. Often, they don't even know.'

'What do Seekers do with them when they find them? Do they kill them?'

'No, no, silly.' Dad chuckled and rubbed my cheek. 'There's a ceremony. If we perform it on the Loki, only his or her powers will be destroyed.'

'Is Mum a Seeker too?' I'd then asked.

He'd nodded. 'She's the best there is.'

'Then I want to be a Seeker too,' I'd told him excitedly.

He'd nodded and hugged me tightly. 'Mum and I will help you.'

But, three weeks later, Mum and Dad were killed in a fire. A fire Sinjin Fury pulled me from. A fire the sorcerer started.

'Why monsters?' Simon interrupts my ponderings.

I turn to him. 'Sorry?'

'Don't be. Why did Fury pick Glumsnappers and Dorfmorons to be in his army and not, say – fluffy kittens?'

I rub my eyes. This boy is so odd. 'Well,' I finally say, 'a fluffy kitten army's not very frightening, is it.'

'No, but...'

I sigh; considering the word 'but' upsets him so much, it's odd how often he utters it.

'...they'd be frightened of hurting the kittens. So frightened, they'd be too frightened to attack. The kitten army wins!'

'There is a sort of logic there,' I admit, 'but I think they'd just, y' know, step on them.'

'STEP ON THEM!' yelps Simon, looking aghast. 'On fluffy kittens!'

'Well, I'm not saying I'D step on them. I'm just saying – oh, forget it.'

We fly over a tiny town of red-slated roofs and zigzagging streets. It reminds me of Lego with hundreds of toy cars chugging along on grey strips of plasticine. All I need to do is pick everything up and throw it in a box.

'A puppy's also very sweet,' the boy mutters, 'and so's a bunny...'

'Simon,' I interrupt him; I keep my hands in my pockets to stop myself from strangling him, 'how did you end up in Devil's Ash?'

'It's a long, long story.'

'I'm listening.'

'OK. Get comfy then.'

'How? I'm in a wicker basket.'

He shrugs. 'First, I hid in a lorry. It took me to Devil's Ash. I met Doris. She took me on.'

I frown. 'And?'

'And – WHAT?'

'And – that's it? Nothing to add?'

'No.'

'Not so long then.

Simon shrugs. 'It seemed long when it was going on.'

'I'm starving,' I suddenly say.

'Here,' He pulls a packet of Cheesy Wotsits from his pocket and offers it to me.

'Thanks.' I rip it open and stuff three in my gob. 'Where did you get them from?'

'The pub cellar.'

I frown at him. 'You were being hunted by Fury and you stopped to grab a packet of Cheesy Wotsits?'

'Three,' he says, pulling two packs from his pocket. He drops them by my feet.

'How did you escape, by the way?'

'There's this tiny door down there. It's how the brewery deliver stuff. Nobody knows it's there but for me and Doris. Oh, and Roger, the delivery driver. There's no proper lock, just a bolt, so I pushed it open and scarpered. I only got fifty feet when I bumped into the Rufus-fellow. He told me to stay with Steel. Then he and this third fellow went off to help you.'

'What did you do with Doris, the landlady?'

'Oh, I told her to hide in a barrel.'

I nod. 'Good thinking.' I finish the first of the

Cheesy Wotsits and I eye his pocket expectantly. 'I don't suppose there's a full English fry up in there, is there? I'd kill for a Ketchup and runny egg butty.'

'I don't like runny eggs,' Simon says. 'They frighten me.'

'Oh. Why?'

'They look runny.'

I nod. 'Yes, they do. Tell me, is that all that frightens you?'

'Oh no, I'm also pternophobic, lutraphobic, genuphobic, blennophobic, chorophobic and asymmetrophobic.'

'Sorry?'

'I'm frightened of being tickled, otters, knobbly knees, slime, dancing and all things assymetrical.'

'Golly!' I look to him in astonishment. 'How do you even sleep?'

'I sleep perfectly well. I'm not frightened of sleep. That'd be silly.'

I roll my eyes. 'I'm a chocoholic,' I tell him with a grin. 'If I see a Twix my knees go wobbly and I begin to dribble.'

'That's different,' he says snootily. 'That's just being a pig.'

For the rest of the morning, we fly on, skirting over ships and jumping dolphins. With a little help from a spell I know, the balloon is flying at jet-like speeds and, soon, we spot Iceland on the horizon.

'Why here?' asks Simon, as we drop lower, flying over the island's rocky cliffs.

'The Sorcerers' Covern is hidden here.' I keep

174

my eyes peeled. Fury knows where I'm going so, if he's going to try and stop me, this is where he'll do it. 'It's just by Gullfoss,' I tell the boy. 'It's a....'

'Waterfall. Yes, I know. I'm very clever. Did you know, fifteen percent of this island is covered in ice and there's only a few trees. It's summer now so it'll be pretty green. This is a volcanic island so there will be lots of bubbling mud pools. Geyser's here too. It's a hot spring. It erupts every few hours but, if you throw a rock in it, it'll erupt sooner.'

I did know this; I was born here, but I just smile and nod.

Simon sighs and begins to twiddle his thumbs. 'Mum got very ill,' he suddenly says. 'She'd promised to get me the October, 1969 Star Trek

175

comic. It's so difficult to find but she'd promised. Anyway, she got mixed up and got me the October, 1996 comic. It's very different-looking. On the front of the 1969 comic, there's a green monster but on the 1996 comic there's a green monster with a yellow, puss-filled zit on his chin. I got so upset.' He gulps. 'So upset, I wished for...' He stops.

'I know,' I say soberly.

He's silent for a moment, still twiddling his thumbs. 'Then, "Where's your mum and dad?"'

'They were killed.'

'Killed?'

I nod. 'By Sinjin Fury.'

'Oh. Why?'

'I don't honestly know but my parents were powerful Seekers and I think Fury thinks this

176

power runs in the family, in me. I think he hoped I'd help him do,' I shrug, 'whatever it is he's planning to do.'

'But why did he kill them?'

'He knew they'd never allow it.'

Silently, the island slips under us, a jigsaw puzzle of green-carpeted hills dotted with rocks and the odd crooked tree. It is summer now but in winter, I know, everything will be hidden by snow.

'We were in China,' I say. 'Mum and Dad were on a job there and they took me with them. Sinjin Fury was there too. The three of them were trying to discover if Attila the Hun was a child of Ammit.'

Simon puts up his hand.

'Mop, this isn't school. Just ask.' His hand

stays up. 'OK,' I say with a sigh, 'what is it?'

'Did you say Attila the Hun?'

'Yes.'

'But he ruled China in...'

'The 13th Century. Yes, I know. I met him. Horrible fellow. He kept murdering everybody. That's why the Sorcerers' Covern suspected he was related to Ammit.'

'And was he?'

'Surprisingly no. He was just a bit of a git.'

'Oh.'

'Anyway, we were living in the hills in a straw hut. But, on the third night, it burnt down and my Mum and Dad were killed. Sinjin Fury pulled me free.'

'Wow!'

'He set the fire too.'

'Oh.'

'But I didn't know it then. So I went with him to Japan and he showed me how to be a Seeker.'

Simon eyes me for a second, a frown hovering over his brow. 'So a Seeker can travel in time?'

I nod. 'Using a Cronus Mirror.'

'Like Doctor Who.'

'Sorry, Doctor – who?'

'A joke?'

'No.'

Suddenly, the boy grins wildly. 'You know, there's a lot of time travelling in Star Trek.'

'Now there's a surprise,' I reply evenly.

'In the seventh film, there's this Borg ship – well, when I say 'ship', it's sort of a cube...'

But, thankfully, I'm saved from the A to Z of

179

Star Trek films by a flaming arrow zooming by my cheek and scorching my left eyebrow.

I pull my wand and look up. There, shadowing the balloon, is a dragon. It is the most horrifying of monsters with a scaly, crusty jacket and the powerful-looking jaws of a scrap car crusher. His black eyes crackle and spark as if he's just swallowed a thunder storm and his claws look capable of ripping a rhino in two.

I spot there is a man saddled to the dragon's back, a second blazing arrow fixed in his bow. It is Fury!

'MAYDAY! MAYDAY!' hollers Simon. 'Help! HELP!' He drops to his belly, gluing his chin to the basket floor. 'But, but – dragons only exist in books,' he stammers hysterically. 'The Lord of the Rings, Harry Potter book two, book three, no, no, book two, book six, book...'

'Mop,' I growl, 'get a grip.'

Fury kicks the dragon brutally in the ribs and the winged-monster drops lower, raking the balloon with his claws.

Wobbly-kneed, I brandish my wand. 'Jellyify!' I bellow. I'm sort of hoping the spell will turn his claws to a mushy sort of goo but it just seems to upset him.

With a snarl, the dragon drops even lower and eyes me scornfully. Then a jet of red sparks erupts from his nostrils.

'Holy cow,' I yelp, scurrying back.

'It's not a cow,' bellows Simon who is curled up by my feet, 'it's a ruddy big...'

'I know, Mop,' I hiss. 'I know.' I elect not to tell him the basket is now on fire.

We must be dropping terribly fast, the wind howling, the punctured balloon pitching and rolling like a crazed bull. Urgently, I look to Simon. 'If we hit too hard, we'll be killed.'

'We must throw stuff over,' the boy hollers back. 'Then we'll be lighter.'

I look frantically to my feet but the basket's empty but for the two bags of Cheesy Wotsit crisps. Simon, I see, is now up on his knees and is eyeing me thoughtfully. 'You must be what – 48 kilos?'

'Don't even think it,' I snarl.

Then, ripping off my boot, I hurl it at the dragon. 'GET LOST!' I cry. But the winged-monster just snaps it up and swallows.

'I don't think the odor of your smelly feet is going to kill it,' says Simon evenly. He sniffs then frowns. 'But, then, it might.'

'Then you try,' I growl.

CRASH!

The balloon hits the top of a tree, softening the blow, and Simon and I are thrown to to the floor in a spaghetti-tangle of arms and legs.

The seconds tick slowly by.

Then, slowly, we clamber up. But, before anybody has a chance to say 'Ow!' or 'I peed my knickers', the monster drops down and begins to gobble up the corner of the basket.

We look on, sort of hypnotised, watching him chew.

Suddenly, Simon picks up a snapped branch and hands it to me. 'Throw it,' he says evenly.

'Sorry?'

'Don't be sorry.'

'No, I – I'm not, I...'

'Just throw – IT!'

I roll my eyes. If I don't, I know he'll never shut up.

Flexing my hand, I narrow my eyes. 'Let's see if I can hit him on the...'

'No, not AT the dragon,' whispers Simon, flapping his hands. 'Over there.'

'OK, OK,' I hiss and I lob the stick away. We watch it cartwheel over a hill of rocks and then land with a splash in a river.

'Fetch it!' hollers Simon. 'Go on, FETCH!

With jaw to chest, I look on. 'Mop, he's not a ruddy dog.'

For a long, LONG second, the monster simply

looks annoyed, hissing softly. Then, much to the fury of the sorcerer, he swoops away to hunt for the stick.

'Wow,' I mutter. 'I'm speechless.'

'Seventy-three percent of animals will fetch a stick if you throw it for them,' Simon informs me.

'Why?'

'They think it's food. Oh, by the way, to be speechless, you must stop talking.'

Suddenly, the branch the basket is sitting on, snaps. We plummet, hitting the dirt with a crunch. The basket tips over and I cartwheel out, thumping my eye on a protruding rock. I see stars then...

...everything turns black.

JAPAN

5th December, 1227 A.D.

Fury's ninja students, boys mostly, had returned to the temple in the beginning of December and I had been truly astonished to see how many he had. Young too, most of them only six or seven years old, and not only from Japan. Many of the labels on the trunks had Italy, Germany, even Peru or China written on them.

After a sixteen hour day of Ninja School, they all seem to be sleeping. Seem to be, anyway, for one of them is only faking it and my job is to discover who it is before he puts a sword to my jugular.

This is my third night on the trot and so far, no luck. Or so Fury thinks. The ninja, I see, is over by the dormitory door; I think he is hoping for just a tiny bit of progress. I grin. He's not going to be a happy chappy then.

In fact, I always know which boy it is, but after destroying the dummy so successfully, Fury now knows how good I am with my fists. I don't want him to discover my other skills.

Now I know he killed my parents, the only thing I can think of is revenge. So it is important he not know how truly skilled I'm becoming. Then, when I strike, I will have the advantage.

With a lantern clutched tightly in my hand, I

tiptoe up to the first bed. The boy, I see, is lying on his belly and dribbling on his pillow. I smile and skulk over to the next lumpy hill. This fellow has the raspy snore of a baby hippo, but it is a little uneven and - I scowl, my bottom lip clamped in my teeth - did I just see his nose twitch?

Cocking my head like a wary sparrow, I let my eyelids flutter shut. THUMP! THUMP! THUMP! THUMP! To me, even from six feet away, the boy's chest thunders with the urgency of a war drum. A new and very handy skill I now seem to possess.

So this is the boy, then. But I do not confront him. On the contrary, I keep my sword in my belt and creep on.

I stop by the third bed and rest my shoulder

on the wall. This boy's a little older, fourteen perhaps with spotty cheeks and a nest of chins. I watch his chest; up and down, up and down. A boy in slumber; he must be in the land of nod. I look by my feet and spot his trunk, 'Jomo' handwritten in red ink on the label.

Confident this is not the lad I'm after, I pretend it is, and I press the tip of my cutlass up to his cheek. 'Got y',' I murmur. I look over to Fury but all I see is the shiny steel of a ninja short-sword.

The second bunk is now empty. As I suspected, it had been the baby hippo. The boy winks at me and, with a chuckle, he lowers his blade and slips off back to his bed.

Under me, Jomo's eyes flicker open and he is momentarily startled. 'Not me! Not me!' he yelps.

Then he sees who it is and thankfully he seems to twig what is happening. 'The ninja skills of a humpless camel,' he murmurs sleepily. He rubs his temple, yawns and shuts his eyes.

By tomorrow, the story of my third unsuccessful attempt will be all over Hornet Temple. 'Incompetent fool!' the other students will cry. 'Why is she even here?' In fact, just what I want them to say. They don't know I'm to be a Seeker. They don't even know what a Seeker is. But they will soon discover how risky it is to think a dozing wolf has no teeth when I turn on Fury.

I pull my sword away from Jumo's cheek and slump dejectedly over to the sorcerer. 'It's just too difficult,' I tell him, the fib slipping off my lips like jelly off a dessert spoon.

For a moment or two, he eyes me pityingly. Then with a belittling, 'TUT!' he grabs my lantern. 'I'm not a fool, Izzy,' he says starchily.

He twirls on his heel and I watch him stomp off down the corridor. Eventually, he turns a corner and I'm left in pitch blackness.

No matter; I can see anyway. Another handy skill I now seem to possess.

J A P A N

With the skills of a ninja, I hop up on a rafter in the roof. Then, when the door opens I allow Felix to walk under me. He lumbers over to my bed, his devilish-red mop of wiry curls all skew-whiff and flattened to the back of his skull. Somersaulting to the floor, I land silently and, quickly, I shut and lock the door.

No boot in the ribs for me today.

I discover Fury in the Rimankyu Room sipping

from a cup. I spot a second pillow on the bamboo floor. He must be expecting me, but then our six o'clock ritual chitchat is now almost three weeks old. I note there's no third pillow. I suspect he knew I'd better his thug.

He is holding the photo of a boy but, when he sees me, he slips it into the folds of his robe. 'Sit, Izzy. Kumis is terrible for the mind but excellent for the stomach.'

Thanking him, I fold my knees, perching on the free pillow. I watch him put a match to two incense sticks, a mix of lemon and...

I sniff the curling smoke.

...cherry wood?

'No Felix,' Fury begins. I spot deep shadows under his eyes. I suspect my tutor did not sleep too well. 'I can only presume then that you locked him in your room.' He balloons his cheeks. 'That's every day this week. He will be awfully upset.'

I nod. The smell from the sticks is potent and I feel my eyelids begin to droop. 'Then Felix must find a different spot to park his boot in the mornings.'

The sorcerer smirks and drinks from his tumbler. He understands cruel humour. 'Indeed he must.'

I feel almost comfortable with this man now. Uncomfortably so, for I know he is a murderer, a man of no morality. A man I'm determined to destroy.

'Why is the Seeker school here in Japan in the 13th Century?' I suddenly blurt out,

He eyes me thoughtfully and I'm confident he

will not tell me. He's a ninja, after all. A man of secrets. Then, suddenly, his lips curl up. 'I was born in 1182 A.D on Shokuku, a tiny island just of Japan. When I was just a boy of six, my father packed me and my two brothers off to the best ninja school on the island.'

He's whispering now and I wonder why. Is he frightened there's a spy in Hornet Temple? But if there is, who is he and who's he spying for?

'In a matter of months I could shoot arrows, climb walls and purposefully dislocate my shoulder to slip free of a knotted rope.

'Then, on my 16th birthday, I was given with the job of murdering the owner of a rival ninja school. My final test. If I succeeded, I'd be Genin, a ninja agent.'

'Did you do it?'

'If I had not, Izzy, I very much doubt I'd be sitting here telling you the story.

'Unfortunately, there was a boy in my school who was very upset he had not been chosen for the job. In a fit of rage, he went to the rival school and told them who'd committed the murder. So, I chopped off the boy's tongue and my family went on the run.'

Blimey! This is not a man to cross, which is a little disconcerting as I totally intend to cross him.

Fury rubs his eyes, perhaps trying to rub away the memory. 'We escaped to the north of Japan and there we met up with Seekers. There's magic in my family so we knew they existed. We decided to work for them.'

'So your brothers left with you?'

'Yes, and no. My younger brother did; he now works for the Sorcerer's Covern too, but my elder brother, he, er – well, he decided to stay. I do not know what happened to him.'

'So then you set up this school in Hornet Temple.'

He nods. 'We tutor boys in the skills of the ninja and, if the Sorcerers' Covern wish it, we secretly help Seekers to be – better Seekers.'

'So the boys here, they never get to know why I'm here? Or where – or when I'm from?'

'No, never.'

'A few months ago, when we met, you were working with Mum and Dad in my century. Why? Isn't it your job to work here, not to go off Seeking?'

Like a stepped-on cobra, the tip of his tongue

darts to his lips. My interest in him is making him jumpy. 'Izzy, I will tell you the rest of my life story the day I trust you.'

'When I pass the ninja test and I'm a Genin too?'

'No.' He smirks evilly, his eyes full of secrets. 'Then the Sorcerer's Covern will trust you. I'm ninja, I trust nobody.'

I shrug indifferently, shifting a little on my numb bottom. How terrible it must be to spend your days trusting nobody. No wonder he drinks so much; the bottle is there to keep him company.

'You impress me, Izzy,' Fury chews thoughtfully on his bottom lip, 'yet you confuse me too. You climb like a monkey and your skill with the sword is almost superhuman; I still wonder how it is you were not killed when you fell from Devil's Fork. No cuts, not even a broken bone. To put it mildly, Felix was very upset.'

'I bet,' I snarl. 'The snake attempted to murder me.'

'No! No!' His eyebrows arch hawkishly. 'He just plays a little rough.'

I snort and violently stir my drink. Then I lift my finger to the cut on my cheek. It's stopped hurting now but I suspect it will be there for the rest of my life. A reminder to never trust anybody. 'He's evil,' I mutter, 'and I will never bow to evil.'

'Interesting,' says Fury, nodding slowly. 'I find 'never' to be a very long time.' We sit silently for a moment, then, 'But for all my tutoring, you still will not jump the pond and you insist you cannot tell who is asleep and who is not. I wonder if, perhaps, my student is not trying to trick me.' He puts his hands together as if in prayer. 'Possibly you wish me to underestimate you. If this is so, then you underestimate me.'

Widening my eyes innocently, I sip from my tumbler. The kumis, a mildly alcoholic drink fermented from cows' milk, is thick and creamy. Fury drinks too, his third glassful.

The ninja rubs his chin thoughtfully then blankly tells me, 'Gojo-Goyuko.'

I scowl. I think he expects me to know what it is. 'Venom,' I propose tentatively, 'or a, er, blowfish soup...'

'No, Izzy,' he sucks in his cheeks, 'it is the Japanese word for the study of the flaws of the enemy.'

'Oh, yes. I see.' I nod wisely, trying to look as if this would have been my third guess.

The sorcerer rubs his temple and ploughs on. 'If the enemy is a coward, or too kind perhaps, or maybe just has a terribly short temper, a clever ninja can turn this on him, exploiting his Achilles' heel.' Fury's eyes twinkle. He enjoys sermonising. 'Using a bribe, flattery or a well thought out insult, the ninja can prod the enemy into doing whatever he wants him to do. You see, Izzy, by understanding the enemy's flaws, he can be easily manipulated and controlled. That is Gojo-Goyuko.'

I steeple my fingers under my chin and mull his words over. Felix had told me on Devil's Fork what my Achilles' heel is: the need to help, to be the hero, and his knowledge of it had almost killed me.

Fury sighs audibly and begins to suck on his teeth. I think my inability to instantly accept his wisdom annoys him immensely. 'Allow me to offer an example,' he mutters, frustration echoing in his words.

I nod. Fury is a monster, but he's also a very talented storyteller and his fanciful yarns usually keep me rooted to my pillow. He swills his mouth with kumis and then swallows; he also drinks too much.

'A powerful ninja is given the responsibility of murdering thirteen of his master's political opponents. Now, this assassin is a very intelligent chap. He looks down the list and sees Lord Nin Po is on there, third from the bottom. The ninja knows this lord to be a very kindly sort and very popular with his followers. He also knows if he is to succeed and kill all thirteen men on his list, he must murder Nin Po first.'

My storyteller cocks his eyebrow and I nod my understanding so far.

'So, the ninja, confident in Nin Po's kindly ways, sits by the door to his castle and pretends to be a leper. The next day, on his way to temple, the lord spots the leper, walks over to him and drops a penny in his lap. The ninja jumps up and thanks him with the swipe of his sword. The assassin then allows himself to be captured and under torture, he surrenders his twelve co-conspirators.'

He looks to me with a quizzical eyebrow.

Reluctantly, I nod. 'They were not his twelve co-conspirators; they were his other twelve targets.' I see the logic in the ninja's plan but still there is no honour in trickery.

'Just so!' Fury claps his hands, no doubt misinterpreting my understanding for agreement. 'The clever ninja knew how much the lord's followers adored him and he correctly judged they'd avenge his murder. They did the rest of the ninja's job for him.'

'I admit it's a clever ploy,' I murmur, 'but it's still cowardly.'

'No, Izzy,' Fury counters with a flaring of his nostrils, 'not cowardly, smart. Remember, only emperors can enjoy the luxury of morals, ninja can only ever enjoy beef stew and cold beds.'

'But I'm going to be a Seeker,' I snap back crossly. 'Anyway, honour is important too, even to a ninja. The lion is worshipped, not the cheetah.'

'Perhaps, but the cheetah brings terror and with terror there is respect.'

'I think maybe Master Fury is confusing respect with...'

Annoyingly, the sorcerer shows me the mollifying palms of his hands. 'Izzy, we can ponder the ins and outs of morality tomorrow. Now, however, we must look to our job for today.' He hops athletically to his feet and, crossly, I scramble up to follow him, bringing my drink with me. It seems, in Hornet Temple anyway, his word is law. There is no room for debate. I wonder, perhaps, if he is frightened I will find a gaping hole in his cold, hard logic.

He escorts me over to a low bench. On it there is a hotchpotch of ninja equipment: I spot a rope and grapple, a pile of throwing stars, even a few caltrops or tetsubishi: sharp metal barbs which, if thrown on the floor, will impale the feet of any unsuspecting enemy. Very nasty!

On the floor, under the bench, I spy two small wooden barrels. Fury shows them to me. 'For three months I have schooled you in the skills of the ninja. You now know the bow, the sword and,' his lips curl up, 'the fists. Now, I must school you in the specific skills of the Seeker.' He pulls a hollow pumpkin from the first of the barrels. 'And we will begin with this.'

Chapter 11

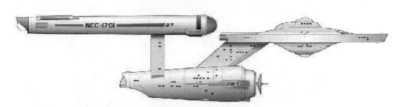

JIGGLING TURNIPS

The wheels of the cart bump over a rock but I don't slow down. Hooking my feet under the lip of the bench I'm sitting on, I whip the pony's rump. 'Go!' I cry. 'GO!' I turn to Simon who is trying to hold on too up to his knees in jiggling turnips. 'We must get to Gullfoss,' I yell.

'Is there not a – smoother way?' he whimpers.

'Yes,' I admit, with a tiny smile, 'but Fury knows it too so we can't risk it.'

He nods. Well, I think he nods. That, or the cart's simply jerking him up and down. 'This way is a lot safer,' I tell him, 'even if it's a bit, er – bumpy.'

'Bumpy!' Simon howls back. 'BUMPY! A toffee whirl's bumpy. A Gorn's skin is bumpy. Star Trek, Episode 18, if you didn't know.'

'Oddly, I didn't,' I reply with a chuckle. I turn to look at him. Poor Mop. I feel sort of sorry for him. It can't be much fun swimming in mushy turnips. But things will not be better for him in Gullfoss. Not by a long way. 'Just hold on,' I holler.

'To – WHAT!?' A turnip? How's that going to help?'

Luckily, we landed by a turnip farm and the farmer there had very kindly let us borrow his pony and cart. Well, when I say 'borrow'; we nicked it.

It's now midday and there's been no sign of Sinjin Fury or his winged pet. But, now, there is a new enemy. The wind. Howling and whistling, it throws up dust making it difficult to see. The cart is slowing too, the pony battling to tow us up a steep hill. Her chin is almost scuffing the dirt and, every so often, she trips. I wonder if, any second now, she'll keel over.

To my left, there is a sudden howl. I twist to look and spot another pony and cart nestled by a rock. To my horror, I see it is crowded with Glumsnappers.

I turn and dig Simon in the ribs. 'Look!' I cry, but he's spotted them too. I whip the pony. 'Go, girl. GO!'

The enemy is moving too, trying to cut us off. And, if we don't hurry, they'll succeed.

'STOP!' yells Simon. 'GO BACK!'

'NEVER!' I trumpet back. I grit my teeth and feel my cheeks redden. 'We can win this.'

'IT'S NOT A RACE!' the boy howls.

Harshly, I whip the pony. 'Yes it bloody well is,' I mutter.

The Glumsnappers hit the path just as we trundle by them. Then, two things happen. An arrow hits my bench and I'm showered in splinters. I yelp, clutching for my leg. Gulping, I look down. My hand is dripping with blood. Then, the two carts collide. Thankfully, we seem to be going the faster of the two and we bulldoze them out of the way-

Closing my eyes to the throbbing in my leg, I

210

twist my body so I can see them. The driver is spinning the cart, whipping his pony on the rump.

Simon jerks my sleeve. 'They don't seem to be giving up.'

'I know,' I yell. 'Evil, mad-dog killers never do.' Then I say two very distressing words. 'Oh no!'

'Don't just say 'Oh no!',' Simon yells. 'Tell me why y' saying 'Oh no!'.'

'How's this? Blisteringly hot toxic mud pools. Better?'

'No.' He shuts his eyes tightly. 'No, no, no, no...'

'OK, I'm lying.'

He peeks and he sees I'm not.

The canyon in front of us is pitted with hundreds of browny-yellow pools. Fizz! Froth! Bubble! Churn! And the stink is stomach-churning.

In terror, I swing the cart over trying to dodge the lethal pools. This is crazy, I think. Bonkers! If the pony slips and we plummet in, we will be cooked like lobsters: very, very crispy.

I clamp my bottom lip in my teeth, tasting blood. Shall we try to jump for it or not? Not! If we do, the Glumsnappers will be on Simon in a second.

I spot two colossal mud pools coming up fast. There's a gap between them but it's much too narrow for the cart.

But I do not stop.

'ISABELLA!' Simon yells, clutching for my sleeve and almost ripping a hole in it. 'THIS IS CRAZY!'

I nod, whipping the pony harshly on the rump.

'Yes, it is.' Like a stampeding bull, we charge. The muddy pools seem to snatch at the wheels, throwing up a flurry of hot mud.

Then in two seconds of blind terror and utter panic, we fly past them. The mud pools, sulky and upset, fizz crossly in our wake.

But, in a FLASH, the Glumsnappers erupt from the maze of mud pools too and I know the hunt is still not over.

I look to Simon, up to his knees in jiggling turnips and a candle splutters to life in my mind. With my fist pressed to my poorly leg, I winch my feet over the bench and drop to the juddering wood.

'You seems to be bleeding,' he informs me dryly.

'Yes, I know.'

'Is it hurting?'

'Yes,' I reply, 'it is.'

'Oh.'

With his show of empathy seemingly over, I pick up a turnip and hurl it at the Glumsnappers' cart. It is only fifty feet away but I miss – badly. 'Help me then,' I cry.

Snatching up a turnip, he lobs it at the chasing wagon. He is a surprisingly good shot and hits a Glumsnapper in the belly. 'Bullseye!' he hollers. Then he turns to me. 'I win,' he says with a smirk.

'I, er – don't think so,' I retort, picking up a mammoth turnip and hurling it at the monsters. But, with a howl, a Glumsnapper swings his sword, splitting the turnip in two.

The rest of the Glumsnappers cheer – but not

214

for long. Thankfully, a lump of the severed vegetable hits the monsters' pony and the driver is forced to pull her up.

Fumbling for the bench, I jump back up on it. 'I think we slowed them up a bit,' I tell the boy.

'But not for long,' he mutters.

I nod. Not for long.

Suddenly, I spot a nest of rocks. 'I'm going to jump off,' I tell Simon.

'But, but – WHY!?'

'Ambush,' I say simply. 'They'll never know what hit them.'

'And what will I do?'

'Just keep going north. Geyser is only a mile or so from here. It's on the way to Gullfoss. If you keep going, you'll soon get there.'

'But...'

'Don't worry,' I try to comfort him. 'I'll be OK. I'll meet you there.'

He nods. 'OK,' he musters. Then, 'Thanks for trying to help me.'

Surprised, I grin. I know it's difficult for him to say this. 'No problem, Mop. I'm a Seeker. It's my job.'

Tossing him the whip, I jump. My feet hit rock and I roll, fire mushrooming from my knee. Then, gritting my teeth, I struggle to my feet.

'Keep low,' yells Simon.

I nod. I intend to. I wonder when — if, we will soon meet. He is suddenly, oddly, very important to me.

Pulling my wand, I run over to the rocks I'd seen. There, I drop to my knees. Not a second too soon for, suddenly, there is the thump of

216

hoofs in the dirt.

I empty my mind of Simon, Sinjin Fury and the Seekers he's murdered. Then, ever so slowly, I peer over the top of the rocks. I see the Glumsnappers and gently, very gently, I twitch my wand.

BOOM!

A deer bolts, a swarm of birds fly up, and a Glumsnapper drops with a yelp to the path. With howls of surprise, the rest of them jump off the cart and run for cover, ducking in amongst the rocks.

The trick is to fire and crawl, fire and crawl; the enemy will soon think he's fighting a shadow.

217

Sadly, my knee's killing me and I possess the agility of a baby with a bucket of bricks. With arrows whizzing over me, I drop to my belly and shuffle over to a nettle patch. A twig snaps, I kick over a rock. Then, ignoring the stings, I nestle down in it.

I stay perfectly still. Listening. Forever listening...

A grunt!

Over to my left.

Slowly, I swing my wand, my eyes on a trembling gorse bush. I spot a Glumsnapper peering over the top...

BOOM!

He grabs for his chest and falls to the dirt.

I drop low and, on my hands and knees, scamper away. A second later the nettle patch I had been hiding in is smattered with arrows.

This is crazy. There is no way I can stop all of them. Then I spot the Glumsnapper's pony and cart.

Scrambling to my feet, I hop up on a rock, jump and land crookedly on the bench. 'GIDDY UP!' A brutal whip and, to the urgent yells of my enemy, we sprint up the path. Only three of them left, I think grimly. Much better odds.

I see curling mist coming from just over the hill; it must be Geyser. I shoot a look over my shoulder. Glumsnappers can run like the wind and my enemy is only thirty feet behind me, looking grim and determined in my dust.

Speeding over the top of the crest, I spot Simon. 'GO, BOY!' I howl, whipping the pony's rump. Trotting up next to him, I jump, landing cat-like on Simon's bench.

'I'M BACK!' I cry.

It is then, with only a hundred feet to go, I spot Fury.

A Thunder Spell hits the wheel, splintering it in two. We lurch over and Simon is sent flying. I follow him but, hitting the dirt, I roll and hop to my feet.

Instinctively, I hunt my pockets for my...'Oh no,' I mutter. 'MY WAND!' Dismally, I peer down at the broken bits. 'Now I'm in the..'

'Where is he?' I look up to see Fury and Felix strolling over. They stop by the boy, who is still sitting in the dirt. 'Up, up,' the sorcerer orders him.

Trembling, the boy gets to his feet.

'Simon, is it?' says Fury, grinning wildly down at him.

'Yes,' whispers the boy with a nervy gulp.

Fury's owlish eyes, tinted yellow from the sun, look doubtfully on the trembling boy. Then he shrugs. 'There's a little job I need help with. Just a tiny, tiny wish. OK?'

'O – OK.'

'Good. You see, they killed my son and they must pay.'

This is news to me. Then I remember the photo he'd been holding in Hornet Temple. His son!? 'Who did?' I butt in. 'A Seeker?'

'Everybody,' he says simply. 'But soon the world will be free of them. This – PEST!' He spits the word. He grips Simon's chin in his fingers. 'Wish it.'

'On – on who?'

'WERE YOU NOT LISTENING?' howls the sorcerer. 'EVERYBODY!'

Pulling free of Fury's grip, Simon's eyes widen in astonishment. He turns to me. 'Izzy,' he whimpers, 'help me.'

With a growl, I limp over to Fury. 'This must stop...'

'SHUT UP!' yells the sorcerer. He lifts his brolly, hitting me in the chest with a Lightning Spell. With a cry, I crumple to my knees. Then he turns back to Simon. 'Now, where were we?'

'AAA-CHOO!!!'

A frown creeps sluggishly over Fury's brow. Then, with his eyes widening in shock, he spins on his heels.

A dumpy-looking fellow with bushy eyebrows and crimson-red cheeks is strolling over to him. He stops. Then, abruptly, he pulls a snotty-looking hanky from his sleeve and tenderly dabs his nostrils. 'Terrible cold,' he informs the sorcerer.

'Thank God,' I murmur. It's Ogun.

The three Glumsnappers run off and a very jumpy-looking Felix slowly backs away.

But Fury simply snorts. 'Sympathy, Ogun, is not my strength. Agreed Izzy?'

Still kneeling in the dirt, I nod solemnly. 'Agreed,' I mutter.

Ogun nods. 'So I'm told. It's risky for you to return here, Sinijn.'

'I will go where I wish,' retorts Fury. But the

sorcerer looks nervy, his white-knuckled fist clamped to the sword on his belt.

'So be it.' He slips me a tiny wink, 'So Sinjin, is it to be sword or spells?

'Swords.' Fury pulls his steel, Ogun instantly mirroring him

'I will show no mercy,' howls Fury, stepping up to him,

'Mercy is a gift given only by the enlightened,' responds Ogun evenly. 'So, to be honest, I did not expect any.'

The two swords hit. In terror, I limp over to the pony and, gripping hold of the cart's front wheel, I duck down. But there's a sudden thump and I feel the wood judder. Felix! He's hunting me.

The seconds tick by in my jumbled mind.

Where is he now, I wonder. My blood is pumping and my poorly knee feels juddery and no longer up to the job of holding me up. I NEED A WAND!

Hypnotised, I watch Ogun and Fury do battle, a blur of sweeping swords and silvery sparks. Ogun is moving with such speed, I can hardly see him. There is werewolf blood in him. I just know it.

Suddenly, Felix catapults off the cart and lands in front of me. I hitch up my dress and run for it.

Out of the corner of my eye I spot Simon. He is curled up by a rock. I grunt. No help there then.

I stumble over to Geyser, Felix wolfishly on my heels. I stop by the bubbling pool knowing I'm trapped. Slowly, my knees trembling, I turn to

225

my hunter.

'Nowhere to run to?' he snorts, his wand in his claw. He steps up to me.

'This is crazy,' I chirrup.

He steps closer.

'Don't do this,' I beseech him, eyeing the wand in horror.

Suddenly, Simon is by my elbow, a rock clutched in his hand and a knowing smirk on his face.

Felix looks to the rock and seems to twig his plan. 'NO!' he howls, back-peddling.

But, calmly, Simon lobs the rock over his shoulder.

KAPLUNK! It lands with a thump in the bubbling pool

I look to him, uncomprehending. 'Why...?'

Slowly, I drop my eyes to my boots. I scowl. The dirt by my feet is trembling.

'RUN!' yells Simon. Clutching my hand, he pulls me away from Geyser.

With the fury of a volcano, it erupts, spurting blisteringly hot water up into the sky.

I jump over Felix, who's tripped over, and dive under the old cart. With my cheek crushed to the cold rock, I pray feverishly to be back in my bed, Rufus fussing over me.

Then, in the blink of an eye, the thunder of Geyser stops.

Simon winks at me. 'Clever, don't you think? Remember, I told you. If a rock's thrown in Geyser, it will erupt.'

I nod. 'Very clever,' I agree.

Slowly, I struggle to my feet. Everything is

hurting. My knees, my elbows, Even my bottom. Everything! But EVERYTHING is forgotten when I peer over the top of the wheel and see what's left of Felix.

'He looks a little – crispy,' mutters Simon.

I nod. 'Just a bit.'

Then I turn to see Ogun on his knees with Fury standing over him.

'There's Glumweedy's blood in me now,' the sorcerer jeers. 'Now, I'm invincible.' He turns and storms over to Simon. Gripping him by the cuff of his jumper, he throws him to the dirt. 'WISH IT!' he bellows. 'KILL EVERYBODY!'

'Everybody?'

'Yes. Wish for it. Wish for it now.'

'No,' says Simon, stuffing his hands in his pockets. 'Never.'

Fury turns and hits me with a Lightning Spell. I cry out in agony. 'Do it or I will kill her.'

'Don't do it, Mop,' I whimper.

BANG! Another Lightening Spell hits my leg, scorching my skin.

'Stop,' says Simon. 'I – I did it.'

Fury looks at him, his eyes narrow. 'What did you wish for? How will they be killed? A flood? A terrible flu epidemic? Tell me, boy.'

'I wished for this,' he rubs his chest, 'to stop working.'

'Excellent...'

'But I only wished it on me.'

'WHAT!?'

Slowly, I clamber to my feet and hobble over to the boy. He drops to the dirt and I kneel next to him.

The sorcerer looks on in bewilderment.

'That was very brave,' I tell him.

'No,' he mutters. 'It was logical. If I'd wish it on everybody, I'd be killed anyway. My Dad too. But now he'll be OK.'

I rest my hand on his t-shirt. I can feel the thump in his chest slowing.

'I did OK, didn't I?' he mutters.

'Yes, you were wonderful. You stopped Fury from destroying the world.'

Simon titters. 'When Kirk was killed in Star Trek 7, he stopped this evil fellow from destroying a world too. But a different world full of green monsters.'

'Gorns?'

He coughs. 'Yes, lots of Gorns. Lots and lots of...' His body shudders and his eyes flutter shut.

230

I swallow.

It is as if a star has blinked out from my sky. But my frozen soul will not let me weep. All I can do is shut my eyes and press his cheek to my chest. I will miss his crazy smile. 'Forever young,' I murmur.

'Fool,' mutters Fury who is still looking on.

Slowly, I turn to the sorcerer. 'Not now, not tomorrow, but soon, I'll find you. I'll never stop hunting till I do. And when I do, I'll kill you.'

With a sneer, he lifts his wand. 'I don't think so. Not if I...

'FURY!'

The sorcerer twists on his heels. 'No!' he howls. 'NOOOOOOOOOOO!'

J A P A N

20th April, 1228 A.D.

Once more I'm back in the Rimankya Room. It is packed wall to wall with Fury's other students and the ninja who school them in the tricky art of being assassins. Fury is stood next to me and by his feet a poker sits ominously in a bucket of red embers.

'Students of Hornet Temple, today we welcome Izzy to the ranks of the ninja.' The sorcerer looks to me, his eyes tomb-like and

232

cold. 'To begin with, Izzy, you must recite the ninja's vows.' He hands me a scroll. 'Try not to whisper,' he says stonily. 'It's a very big room.'

I nod. Unrolling the parchment, I study the words. Why, I wonder, must I do this. I'm to be a Seeker, not a cold-blooded killer. But Fury is insisting. So, a little reluctantly, I begin, 'I, Izzy Crowl, vow to uphold the laws of the ninja. Firstly, to never be seen by the enemy and never to kill eye to eye. Secondly, when all is lost, run for the hills...' I stop. This is stupid. I will never do any of this.

'There's a third,' mutters Fury. I feel the sorcerer's elbow in my ribs. 'SAY IT!' he orders me.

I sigh. 'Thirdly, to kill when I'm instructed to kill.'

There is a muted cheer and everybody claps. Sort of. Just for a second or two. I don't think they trust me. Clever kids.

With the flamboyancy of a circus clown, Fury pulls the poker from the fire. On the tip of it I spy a red hot lump of iron in the form of a six-pronged throwing star. I clench my teeth. HE PLANS TO BRAND MY WRIST!

I watch him stroll over to me, embers of joy dancing in his devilish eyes.

'This may sting just a little,' he chirrups optimistically.

I swallow, the thought of the red hot stamp on my skin terrifying me. I try to back away but all too soon my bottom hits the tapestry-draped wall. 'You know, I don't mind if you just tattoo it on.' My words rising to a hysterical whine.

'Izzy! Izzy!' He titters pitilessly. 'There'd be no fun in that.'

'But I'm going to be a Seeker, not a...'

He cuts me off by snatching my hand, twisting it and stamping the iron to my tender skin.

My knees buckle and, with a cry, I sink pathetically to the floor. There, I promptly throw up over Fury's feet.

The sorcerer looks on, a smirk playing at the corner of his lips. He's not upset. In fact, I think he thinks he's just discovered my Goyo-Goyuko. FIRE! Unfortunately, I think he's spot on.

'Welcome to the ninja,' he says triumphantly. His eyes flicker momentarily to the window and the pond. 'You never did jump it.'

'No,' I look up, my eyes wild and angry, 'I never did,' I hiss.

Billy Bob Buttons

THE **DAYS** AFTER

TOMORROW

Chapter 12

INK POTS AND PENCILS

Slowly, I tow my feet up to my bedroom. I'm shattered from my work-out, a back-wrenching, muscle-cramping mix of high kicks, jumps, rolls and jabs. Ogun even insisted I do two hundred and fifty frog hops! But it's not just shaky legs and battered elbows cluttering up my mind. It's been weeks and still nobody knows where Fury is or who he's now trying to hunt down.

Stumbling into my room, I thankfully slam the door shut. I sleep in the loft. It is very cosy up here with sloping walls and a wonky floor. When my mum had been a kid, she'd slept in here too. Her tatty books still crowd the bookshelf and Rebecca, her ragdoll, still sleeps in my bed. I see she is sitting up on the pillow, her left eye jammed shut so it looks as if she's winking at me. I pull off my boots and wink back.

I wander over to a stool and drop down. It is still only ten o'clock in the evening and I see the sun is still up, Gullfoss filling my window. Only a hundred or so feet away, the plunging water thunders into the canyon, throwing up a drenching mist and obscuring the hills. Just in front of where I'm sitting is Grandad's shabby, old tool shed, the roof rotten and smothered in moss and, just by it, a flower bed brimming with dancing snapdragons. Soon it will be winter and the flowers will perish. So, if I wish to draw them, I must do it now.

I peer down at the floor. There, by my feet is a pad and a wooden box. The lid is up, showing off a mix of pencils, a brush and six ink pots. The pots sit in two rows of three, a present from my mum on my seventh birthday. She even had 'Isabella' etched on the lid, a flower climbing the leg of the 'I'.

I put the paper on my knee, snatch up a pencil

and begin to sketch. With a sweep of my hand, the jutting stem of the snapdragon is drawn. I find this is the best way to do it; it is important the stem flows and is not jerky or bumpy. The top of the stem bows over to the bell-shaped flowers. Charily, I sketch the borders of the petals and pepper them with dots.

Drawing is how I relax. But, today, it's difficult. My mind is too full of Sinjin Fury. Where is the evil sorcerer and who, I wonder, is he trying to kidnap now.

My sketch is now in need of a little colour. I unstopper the ink pots and dip the brush in the yellow. Soon Fury is blanketed in much sweeter thoughts of snowy-tipped, yellow petals and green-speckled stems. Even the throb of my knee is forgotten.

My mind drifts to Simon and how, with his eyes fluttering shut, he'd winked at me. WINKED! Clever boy. He did not wish for anything. He'd just been pretending. Thankfully, Fury fell for it and, with the injured Ogun on his heels, he'd scarpered. Then, when he'd left, Ogun performed the ceremony and Simon's 'gift' was destroyed forever.

Now, thankfully, the boy is back with his dad in Trotswood and enjoying his nightly fix of Star – whatever it is.

I suddenly feel happy.

Content...

There is a knock at the door, puncturing my happy bubble. 'Yes?' I call.

It opens and I look up to see Ogun. The sorcerer suddenly looks very old, his fingers thin and bony, folds of skin dripping from his cheeks and his dimply chin. I think he's still tired from his fight with Fury. 'We've got him,' he says.

'Who? Fury?'

He nods. 'And he's with a son of Ammit.'

'Where?' I snap, jumping to my feet.

The old sorcerer sighs. 'Not where, Izzy. When.'

I nod. It is as if I'm stood in the street and, any second now, a cement truck is going to knock me over. Reluctantly, I stopper the ink pots, dry off the brush and rest the pad on the pillow to dry.

Now...

I eye my room thoughtfully...

Where's my new wand?

Chapter 13

FLOWERY BONNETS AND MUFFIN MEN

It is frigidly cold in London, the sort of damp, windy day common to the tiny island. A swollen cloud with a droopy belly hovers over the city, keen to wash away the mist and the stink rising up from the river.

My knee is much better now, so I hop off the deck of the Sweeper, a hundred and fifty foot clipper and my taxi all the way from Gullfoss.

Then, with a cheery wave to the crew, I stroll up the dock.

It is still only 6 o'clock in the morning, but the jetty is bustling with pipe-smoking fisherman dropping off barrels of fish; mostly cod and the odd flapping salmon all destined for Billingsgate fish market. The whalish hulls of cargo ships sit anchored to the dock too. Dockers called Lompers and Whippers carry barrels of rum and chests of coffee from the ships' holds to mammoth sheds constructed of driftwood walls and rusty bolts. There, they will be numbered and a tax put on them.

I stop for a second to watch a boy cut the fins of a salmon and skin it. He then throws the flesh to a second boy who cuts it into strips and dips them in a bucket of salt. I'm suddenly reminded of Simon's words to me in his bedroom. 'My life is like drowning fish. Totally impossible.' I balloon my cheeks and stroll on. My life is beginning to feel that way too.

Soon, I spot a car parked up at the top of the dock. It is very elegant-looking with spoked wheels and shiny steel bumpers, a winged angel bolted to the bonnet. I feel my fists curl up. There, slumped by the wheel, is Steel. Ogun did not tell me I'd be working with this slimy git.

He never did find Rufus or Cody; and, to be honest, I don't think he even bothered to try. I suspect he just hid, happy to let me fight Fury on my own.

The volcano in me stirs, but now I know how to control my fury; in Rufus Splinter's words, 'To show the demon who's boss.' I simply think of

244

the flowers I draw, the sweep of the stem, the soft, velvety petals.

On my trip to England, I often pondered this evil in my skull. Is it simply Sinjin Fury playing with me – or, am I the demon? Whatever it is. This need to hurt, to kill even, I will channel it. For now, it is my ally and it will help me to stop Fury ever finding a Loki. Then, when it's over, when Fury is tucked up in his coffin, I will find a way to destroy it.

So, with flower beds of snapdragons firmly entrenched in my mind and the volcano firmly pugged, I march over to the Seeker.

'Hello, Izzy,' he says breezily, hopping from the car. He daps a hanky to his lips but I still spy his rotten teeth. 'Good trip?'

I can smell the hatred in him, festering in his

belly. I know the stench for it sits in my belly too. He knows I know what he is. A coward.

'Very,' I reply curtly.

'Good. Good.' He frowns. 'No trunk?'

'No.' I pull my wand from my pocket and idly finger the tip. 'Just this. It's all I need.'

A tiny sneer widens his nostrils. Then he licks his lips and swallows. 'Hop in. There's a way to go and the traffic's terrible.'

'Where we off to?'

'I booked you a room at the Hilton. It's important you sleep well. Tomorrow, there's a lot to do.'

I nod and we clamber in. 'Do we know where the suspect is?' I ask him.

'Yes,' he says. 'Berlin.'

The doors slam, the motor growls, there is a

clunk and we trundle off.

'So, how's Ogun?' he asks me bracingly. 'Is he still recovering from his fight with Fury?'

I reply with cold eyes and a cold shoulder and turn to wind down my window. I always enjoy my trips into history hunting for the children of Ammit. Now the Cronus Mirror sent me to London in September, 1939. World War Two is just on the horizon and the city has not yet been scarred by German bombs.

With interest, I watch Piccadilly Circus rattle by, a toffee tin box of butchers, aproned-flower sellers and poky shops with windows full of umbrella, flowery bonnets and shiny-buckled ankle boots. I spy a chimney sweep, a ladder hooked to his shoulder, then a muffin man, a wooden platter piled with current buns resting on his cap. Everywhere I see billboards for 'Bovril' and 'Drink Cadbury's Cocoa', and a poster for The Morgue Theatre, a play called 'Roped to a Corpse'.

But it is the smells of the city I enjoy the most. The butchers reek of old blood and rancid fat, the flower sellers of lavender and rose. I get a whiff of soot and porridge off the chimney sweep and, from the muffin man, melted butter and warm ovens.

By my elbow, Steel natters on. But, thankfully, most of his nervy drivel is lost to the clatter of the wheels and the bellows of the butcher boys and flower girls on the street.

'Lamb! Welsh lamb! A penny a leg!'

'Daffodils! A half penny a bunch!'

But I do catch this. 'Yes, yes, tomorrow is a

248

big day. I will fully prep you in the zeppelin on the way to Germany. The suspect is well protected so it will be difficult to kidnap him. But we must try. Then, we will transport him to Gullfoss for the ceremony.'

I scowl. Did he say zeppelin?

'We mustn't dillydally. We think Fury's in Berlin too.'

'How do we know?'

'There's been a lot of, er – thunder storms. And, if Fury gets to him first, well...'

My interest spiked, I turn to the Seeker. I can tell by the playful spark in his eye he's dying to tell me. 'Who is it?' I ask him begrudgingly. 'Who do we suspect is the Loki?'

He smirks, enjoying the power of him knowing and me not. Then, he says, 'Adolf Hitler.'

I feel my eyes spin. I even drool a little. The Sorcerer's Cover expects me to kidnap HIM!

The car's wheels hit a rut with a bone-shaking crunch, perfectly matching the moment.

Then...

...it begins to drizzle.

In my hotel room, I roll over and over on my bed, twisting and turning, clawing at my pillows. In my tortured mind, I suddenly see him.

FURY!

His black eyes crackling and sparking as if

he'd just swallowed a thunder bolt. His cheeks swarming with tiny maggots. His crocodile teeth erupting from car-crusher sized jaws.

A burst of red-hot fury thumps me in the chest and, with a cry, I tumble off my bed and sink to the carpet, my knees to my chin. Curled up like a baby in a womb, I pray for it to stop. I WILL DO ANYTHING! ANYTHING IF IT WILL JUST STOP.

'Now, that is interesting,' the demon in my mind rasps slyly.

FELICITY
BRADY
AND THE WIZARD'S BOOKSHOP

SPECTACULAR!
SCHOOL NEWS

BY THE AWARD WINNING
BILLY BOB BUTTONS